The terrorist snaked an arm around the teenager's throat

Mack Bolan lined the sights of the big .44 on the bridge of the Arab's nose.

"Drop your weapon," Khalid roared, his pistol pressed against his victim's temple, "or I'll kill her!"

"I don't think so," the warrior replied.

"What?" the Arab said, startled.

"If I drop my gun, you'll kill *me*. The fact is, if you don't hurry up and kill her, I'll have to do it myself. She's getting in the way, keeping me from doing my job." The Executioner held the Desert Eagle steady. The angle for the shot was bad. He had less than half an inch clearance over the young woman's shoulder, and less than that to the side of her cheek.

The confidence had drained completely from Khalid's face. The man's eyes flickered right, then left, as if he hoped that one of the corpses on the floor would rise from the dead and come to his aid.

A life hung in the balance. It was now or never.

The Executioner squeezed the trigger.

MACK BOLAN.

The Executioner

DON PENDLETON'S THE EXECUTIONER® FEATURING MACK BOLAN®

WELLFIRE

A GOLD EAGLE BOOK FROM

WORLDWIDE.

TORONTO • NEW YORK • LONDON
AMSTERDAM • PARIS • SYDNEY • HAMBURG
STOCKHOLM • ATHENS • TOKYO • MILAN
MADRID • WARSAW • BUDAPEST • AUCKLAND

First edition September 1994

ISBN 0-373-61189-7

Special thanks and acknowledgment to
Jerry VanCook for his contribution to this work.

WELLFIRE

Be bloody, be bold, and resolute.
> —William Shakespeare,
> *Macbeth*

In every deed . . . he had a heart to resolve, a head to contrive and a hand to execute.
> —Edward Gibbon
> 1737–1794

There is a point beyond which no man will allow himself to be pushed, no matter how meek he may be.
> —Mack Bolan

PROLOGUE

Four of the six men were already dead. The fifth looked to be well on his way.

Willem Gerhardt shoved a fresh magazine into the AK-47 and inched his eyes up over the windowsill. The dazzling lights that hid the German GSG-9 squadron blinded him. He blinked. During the millisecond in which his eyes were closed, a new volley of 9 mm fire from the counterterrorists' H&K MP-5s blasted the remaining glass from the window and drove Gerhardt back to the floor.

He hugged the hardwood floor as what seemed like thousands of rounds flew over his head, drilling into the rear wall of the safehouse and sending a storm of white plaster whirling through the air. He coughed as dust infiltrated his lungs. The onslaught continued, and he turned his head toward the men on the floor.

Brunvand, Roder, Mueller, Schneider. He could see all four, their wild eyes still open in death; their insides spilling from bullet-rent chests.

A low moan of anguish came from the other side of the four bodies. Gerhardt heard Omari whisper a prayer in Arabic. He shifted his gaze to the man. Omari had taken a bullet though the lung. Blood pumped from the hole, and a red froth sprayed from his lips as he prayed.

The assault continued with unrelenting resolve, ripping more plaster from the walls. Bullets tore through a cross beam in the ceiling, and suddenly Gerhardt found himself buried beneath a pile of wooden studs and other debris. Something heavy—a beam, he supposed, came tumbling down on the side of his knee, twisting the joint to the side. He felt the ligaments stretch, and screamed at the pain.

The GSG-9 gunmen lowered their aim. New rounds pummeled into the wall below the window frame. The sandbags piled inside the wall stopped the penetrating 9 mm rounds, but Gerhardt felt the vibration of each round against his shoulder.

His knee still burning, the German dug himself out from under the rubble. How much longer should he try to hold out? Enough food and water was stored inside the safehouse for several days; not that it was likely to do him any good. He was the last gun left, and it was only a matter of time now before a tear gas grenade, or "flash-bang," came hurtling through the window. When that happened, the men outside would rush the house. They would kill him before he had recovered from the shock.

The gunfire died down momentarily, giving the terrorist a chance to consider his options. Surrender now, or continue to fight? The longer he held out, the better the chance that he would be killed.

And getting killed wasn't part of the German's plan.

As the hailstorm continued over his head, the German listened to the continued moans of the man on the floor. His mind flashed back over the past twenty years. He and Omari had been close friends since their initial training, both by the KGB and Carlos the Jackal. The night before, they had sat awake drinking wine, playing backgammon and reliving old times.

Now, Omari might die. On the other hand, Gerhardt had seen men survive worse lung wounds than the Arab appeared to have sustained. Omari might well pull through if GSG-9 got him to medical attention quickly. But if that happened, he would be interrogated.

Which meant the information Willem Gerhardt was prepared to trade for his freedom would be only be *half* as valuable.

The gunfire died down. Gerhardt heard the words over the gas-operated bullhorn as clearly as if they had been shouted into his ear. *"Surrender immediately, or you will die!"*

Without further thought, the German turned the barrel of the AK-47 toward his old friend. His index finger found the trigger.

Omari moaned again, opened his eyes and stared in horror at the man he had fought alongside for more than twenty years.

Gerhardt's mind was already on the steps of safe surrender when he squeezed the trigger and sent a full-auto burst into Omari's face.

The rounds inside the house brought a new assault from the GSG-9's submachine guns. As the bullets flew over his head, Gerhardt ripped the white shirt from his back and pulled it down over the hot barrel of the AK-47.

"Do not shoot!" he screamed as he raised the white flag above the window. "I surrender!"

1

"Love is just a beer away," sang the twanging voice inside the jukebox of Eischen's Bar in Okarchie, Oklahoma. But the man in the chambray Western shirt, faded jeans and shining yellow ostrich-quill boots knew better. Mack Bolan had been sitting at the bar for nearly an hour, and it seemed to him that each beer brought the men in the room closer to violence than it did to love.

Three men in oil-stained work khakis sat around a shuffleboard table at the rear of the room. They ignored the metal disks on the sawdust covered table, concentrating instead on shots of bar whiskey and long-necked bottles of Budweiser. Two of the men looked to be in their late twenties. The third was older, with gray hair peeking out in curls from under the hard hat that covered his head. Their clothes, along with the grime permanently installed under their fingernails and impacted into the skin of their hands, told Bolan they were oil-field hands—probably roughnecks responsible for the care and operation of the rotary engines.

Three more men, smelling only slightly less of crude oil and wearing somewhat cleaner clothes, sat

slouched in a booth against the wall by the jukebox.
Bolan had pegged them as derrickmen who stood on
the "monkeyboard" ninety feet in the air, and han-
dled the upper end of the drill string, drilling fluid,
and the mud pump and mixer. They, too, drank
boilermakers.

The reason for the imminent violence Bolan sensed
stood swaying to the music behind the bar in a tight
orange halter top and black skirt. Bolan had heard one
of the roughnecks call her Lucy Ann, and as he stared
into the mirror behind the bar, the Executioner saw
her grin his way.

At the same time, the mirror showed the scowls on
the male faces behind him.

The reason for the tension in the room was as old as
mankind itself. Like the song said, it concerned love,
but only one aspect of that emotion. It centered primarily on simple lust, with a generous dose of jeal-
ousy thrown in. It pretty much boiled down to the fact
that Lucy Ann and the men in Eischen's were "lo-
cals." Bolan was a stranger. And the oil-field hands
didn't like the attention the barmaid was throwing his
way.

The Executioner checked the mirror, making sure
the angry eyes were no longer watching him, then adjusted the 9 mm Beretta 93-R beneath his shirt. The
clothes he wore offered limited options for carrying a
concealed weapon, so he had resorted to an elastic and
Velcro Bianchi "belly band" around his chest. The
deep-cover rig hid well on a man with wide shoulders
and a narrow waist, its only liability being a slower-
than-usual draw. Bolan had offset that problem with

the snap-closure Western shirt. The snaps could be ripped open in a fraction of a second, permitting almost instant access to the Beretta.

Lifting his beer mug once more, the Executioner took a sip. The beer had grown warm over the past half hour, but he had said no to the barmaid each time she'd offered him a refill. He had also played dumb to her obvious flirtations. He had work ahead of him, and the last thing he needed was a fuzzy brain or the fight that was likely to come if he answered the offer that had already been made by the braless breasts that brushed his arm each time the woman rounded the bar to deliver more drinks to the customers.

As he set his mug back on the counter, the door on the other side of the bar suddenly swung open. Rays of hot Oklahoma sunlight streaked in with the wind. The men at the tables cursed, then silenced themselves abruptly as a tall man in skintight black Western slacks, a red shirt with pearl snaps and a black Stetson strutted in. Black muttonchop sideburns fell almost to the man's chin, emphasizing his pudgy, pasty face. The hair around his ears was matted with sweat, and the red shirt threatened to pop open at the gut that hung beneath a large silver rodeo buckle.

Bolan watched him squeeze onto a stool in front of the telephone at the opposite end of the bar, then turned back to his beer.

The Executioner was going under the name Rance Pollock, an identity he often used when working with the U.S. Department of Justice. And Pollock was waiting for the arrival of a man he had never met, someone named Bob "Roady" Rose. But the fat man at the end of the bar wasn't Rose.

According to Hal Brognola of Justice, Roady Rose was a U.S. Department of Justice agent and a part-time rodeo cowboy. A good warrior, the big Fed had said.

In the mirror, the Executioner saw the barmaid turn to face the man at the end of the bar. "You can't come in here, Lonnie," she said softly. "You know that. Judge said."

"I reckon I can come into any goddamn public business establishment I want to," the fat man said, sneering.

The barmaid shook her head. "Uh-uh. You got to stay a hundred yards away from me, that's what the judge said. We ain't married no more, and I got a re-strainin' order." Her hand moved to her hair and parted it to emphasize her statement.

Bolan saw stitches binding a deep red abrasion together.

The man called Lonnie laughed. "Bring me a Bud, Lucy Ann."

The barmaid shook her head again. "Ain't gonna do it." She reached for the phone, but the fat man's hand shot out with surprising quickness. His fingers locked around her wrist.

The room fell silent.

Lucy Ann's eyes darted immediately to Bolan. The look on her face, as well as the movement itself, told the Executioner all he needed to know about Lonnie.

The woman obviously knew the other men in the room, yet she hadn't looked to them for help. All of the men had cast lust-filled eyes her way as she worked the bar. They wanted her, but they wouldn't stand up to her ex-husband. Which meant, as the old joke went, Lonnie must be the "toughest SOB in the valley."

Bolan watched the fat man tighten his hold. Lucy Ann's face contorted with pain. The Executioner had no desire to get involved in a domestic squabble, particularly when he was about to meet a man who had far more important business for him to attend to. On the other hand, he had never been able to stand passively by while the strong took advantage of the weak.

Lonnie followed the woman's gaze, his gaze stopping on the Executioner. "What you lookin' at, asshole?" he asked Bolan.

The warrior stood slowly and walked to the end of the bar. "How about I buy you a beer?" he said. He tossed a ten-dollar bill on the bar.

Lonnie's eyebrows lowered menacingly. "How about I beat the hell out of you?" he answered.

Bolan shook his head. Reason wasn't going to work. His eyes narrowed. "You don't want a beer, I'll give you another choice. How about you let go of the lady's arm and I won't break yours?"

The shock on Lonnie's face affirmed Bolan's suspicion that the man wasn't used to being challenged. Then the shock changed to an oily, evil smile.

"Back on outta here, mister," said a voice from the rear of the room. "Believe me, you don't want no part of ol' Lon."

Bolan had waited long enough. He reached out, grasped the fat man's fingers and pried them from the woman's arm. Then, continuing to apply pressure against the wrist, he twisted down and out.

A sharp shriek escaped Lonnie's lips as the wrist lock forced him to the floor. His face turned crimson with anger and embarrassment.

The Executioner released the wrist, stepped back and decided to try the peaceful approach again. "I'd still be happy to buy you a beer," he said.

Peace wasn't going to work.

Lonnie leaped to his feet, again surprising the Executioner with his speed. Bolan barely had time to step to the side as the fat man charged, head down.

The warrior dropped a fist, coming up with an uppercut as Lonnie raced by. A crisp crack echoed through the room as bone met bone, then another shriek drowned out the sound. The shriek was replaced with a bullish snort as Lonnie's head snapped up and back, the black Stetson flying from his head.

The Executioner stepped in, driving a hard left into the man's gut. The fat over Lonnie's midsection quaked as Bolan's fist drilled past to the sternum.

Air whooshed from Lonnie's lungs. His eyes rolled back in his head as he tumbled to the floor.

Instincts honed first in the jungles of Vietnam, then street jungles the world over, told the Executioner to duck. A heavy glass beer mug sailed over his head. He turned in the direction from which it had come, and saw the three men in khakis rising from around the shuffleboard table.

The gray-haired man lifted the hard hat from his head to reveal a bald pate. "None of us like ol' Lon much," he said, his steely eyes fixed on the Executioner, "but we don't much care for some goddamn Yankee son of a bitch coming into our bar and whoopin' it up on one of our own, neither." His hand disappeared behind him.

His back against the bar, Bolan waited.

"No fancy-pants Northerner is gonna stroll in here and just take the place over," a stocky younger man growled.

The third man, tall and lanky, charged suddenly, making the same mistake Lonnie had made. Bolan held his ground, catching him with a snap kick to the groin that brought a girlish squeal from the attacker's open mouth. Both hands grasped his crotch as he fell across Lonnie on the floor.

The stocky man ripped his hard hat from his head and stepped in, holding it up as a weapon.

In the corner of his eye, Bolan saw the door open again. Two more men stepped into the bar as the man in the khakis swung the hard hat toward the Executioner's head.

Bolan shuffled to the side. One arm shot up, blocking the hard steel. He bent at the knees, driving a short jab into the stocky man's ribs, then twisted his wrist and brought the same fist up in an uppercut that lifted the roughneck off his feet and dropped him to a sitting position on the floor.

The hard hat clanked off the steel post of a bar stool as it flew from the man's fingers.

Bolan's gaze shifted to the older man.

Slowly the hand that had disappeared into a back pocket returned to the front. Empty.

The Executioner glanced toward the men in jeans in the booth against the wall. One of them smiled nervously and raised his beer. "Don't mind us, feller," he said. "We're from Kansas. Just down here workin' the patch awhile. Ol' Lon don't mean nothin' to *us*." The other two men laughed uneasily.

Bolan turned his attention to the two men who had just entered the bar. His gaze fell on a bareheaded man, of medium height and weight, wearing a tight black T-shirt, jeans and black Western boots. Wiry muscles extended from the shirt's short sleeves—the type of muscles developed by hardworking rodeo cowboys.

The other man was tall and gaunt, with a sallow complexion. Large red knuckles stuck out on his bony fingers beneath the cuffs of his long-sleeved shirt. He, too, wore Western wear, but he looked uncomfortable.

The Executioner noticed he stood with his weight on one leg, as if he might have suffered a recent leg injury. And if his name was Willem Gerhardt, as Bolan suspected, he had.

The shorter man walked up to Bolan and extended his hand. "I'm Roady Rose," he said. "No need to ask who you are, I guess. Our man back in Washington told me about you, Pollock. And what I just saw ID's you better than a driver's licence."

The three men exited the bar without another word.

A black Chevy Blazer with Texas tags stood in the bar's gravel parking lot. As Rose slid behind the wheel, Bolan took the shotgun seat while Gerhardt got into the back.

"I grew up not far from here," Rose said as he keyed the ignition. "Over near Calumet. My daddy was a rancher. Had some oil property, too."

Bolan nodded. "You must have had some money."

"Oh yeah," Rose said. "Oil saw to it. Then we had the cattle and some racehorses. My favorite was a golden palomino. Named him Trigger."

The Executioner smiled. "You have a dog named Bullet, too?"

"Well . . . yeah."

Bolan chuckled. Brognola had casually mentioned that Rose had a Roy Rogers fixation. "So what made you want to be a cop?" he asked.

Rose shrugged. "A man's got to go his own way," he said simply. "But I reckon it was that background made Mr. Brognola pick me for this job. I know the oil patch. Inside and out. Born with crude runnin' through my veins, as they say." He pulled out of the lot and started down the street.

Bolan pulled down the visor, looked up into the mirror attached to the back and studied the man in the back seat. Gerhardt had taken off his cowboy hat to expose a mop of long stringy blond hair. His thin eyebrows looked as if they'd been drawn on his forehead with a yellow pencil, and the eyes beneath them darted back and forth from Rose to the Executioner like those of an anxious ferret.

Hal Brognola had run down the situation to him over the phone only a few hours earlier. Gerhardt had been busted in the takedown of a safehouse outside of Bonn, Germany. Gerhardt, and four of the other terrorists inside, had been members of the Red Army

Faction—the successor to the old Baader-Meinhof gang. But GSG-9, Germany's crack counterterrorist squad, had also discovered the body of an Arab in the house. He had been identified as a free-lance terrorist with strong ties to the Islamic Unification Movement, a Muslim fundamentalist group.

Terrorism had changed over the years, Bolan reflected. It had become as organized as "big business" with international intelligence networking between the different organizations that rivaled, and sometimes surpassed, that of the CIA and similar agencies.

The Executioner shifted in his seat. The bottom line was that Willem Gerhardt had rolled over. He had information to trade for his eventual freedom.

Bolan twisted to face the man in the back seat. "So tell me what's going on," he said to Gerhardt. Even though Brognola had filled him in on the details, he wanted to hear them from Gerhardt himself.

"I told your man in Washington when they first brought me to the U.S.," the German said.

"And now you're going to tell it all again." Bolan had taken an instant dislike to the man—not that he usually had any affection for terrorists. Regardless of the importance of the German's information, or the global implications of the mission, Gerhardt was a murderer. Not only of men, but of innocent women and children as well.

And right now, he was nothing more than a snitch, and snitches, with very few exceptions, could never be trusted not to play both ends against the middle.

Gerhardt had started to speak when Rose turned off the street under a sign announcing the Okarchie Motel. The Justice agent parked in front of a splintered wooden door with a Roman numeral six screwed into the chipped paint. The three men exited the vehicle with Rose leading the way to the room.

The motel was hardly the Beverly Hills Hilton. A crumbling wooden bed covered by a tattered brown bedspread stood against the wall. A scarred metal table held an old black-and-white television. The seats of two steel-framed linoleum-covered chairs had been pushed under the tabletop.

The Executioner motioned Gerhardt to the bed and pulled out the chairs. He dropped into one as Rose took the other.

"So," Bolan said. "Talk."

Gerhardt shrugged. "What do you know about me?"

"Gerhardt, Willem Hans," the warrior said. "Born in Munich, you grew up in West Berlin where you took up with the wrong sort of people. Trained in the former Soviet Union, then Libya." He paused, "So now tell me what you're trading."

Gerhardt crossed his legs at the ankles. "Two nights before the GSG-9 discovered the safehouse in Germany, I learned from one of our Arab comrades that Saddam Hussein is finally planning to carry out the terrorist retaliation on U.S. soil that he has promised since the Gulf War."

"Why now?" Rose demanded. "Why did he wait so long?"

The German pursed his lips and shrugged. "I do not know. Perhaps for several reasons. A new President is in office, and I do not think Iraq fears this man as much as your former leader. Or perhaps Saddam simply wanted to wait until your government's guard was down. In any case, as I am sure your superiors must have told you, what is planned is frightening in its scope." Gerhardt paused, pulled a pack of cigarettes from his shirt pocket, shook one from the pack and lighted it. "He is planning to set several hundred oil wells in Oklahoma aflame simultaneously.

Bolan had learned all that from Brognola. "Go on," he prompted.

Gerhardt took a drag on the cigarette. "I know very little more about that operation, except that it is to be conducted by a force that has united several Muslim freedom-fighting organizations—"

"Terrorists," Rose said at Bolan's side. "Those bastards aren't freedom fighters. They're terrorists."

The German smiled. "As you wish. Regardless of what you call them, Saddam Hussein has united groups from around the world. They are operating under an umbrella organization entitled Istad Itar. Do you know what it means in Arabic?"

Bolan shook his head.

"Return the favor."

"Saddam always was noted for his wit," Rose said sarcastically.

"When's this all set to go down?" Bolan asked.

"Sometime soon. My friend Omari was not definite. But in the next few days, certainly." Gerhardt smiled the smile of a contented wolf.

The Executioner stood. "How do you plan to help if that's all you know?" he said.

Gerhardt shrugged. "I do not know yet. But if you can get a lead into some faction of the operation, there is a good chance I will know someone involved. I could then introduce you as a mercenary friend of mine. You would take over from there, of course."

The warrior walked slowly toward the bed. When he stood directly in front of the sitting German, he stared down at the man.

The smile on the German's face faded, and his gaze dropped to the floor.

Bolan reached down and grabbed the man's shirt-front. With a quick upward thrust, he jerked the terrorist to his feet. "There are a few things we need to get straight up front," he said. "First, I don't take charge after you introduce me. I'm in charge now. Second, any promises of leniency or immunity you got didn't come from me. The only promise I'll make you is that I'll kill you if you try to double-cross me."

"You'll have to beat me to him," Rose growled behind the Executioner. Bolan glanced over his shoulder.

Rose stared at Gerhardt. "I'll put a slug in you faster than you can spit and holler."

The warrior turned back to Gerhardt. "You understand all that?" he asked.

The German's head bobbed in affirmation.

Bolan dropped him back to the bed. Turning to Rose, he said, "I'm going to take the Blazer on into Oklahoma City and see what I can turn up. You baby-sit this guy. You got expense money?"

Rose nodded, tapping the pocket of his jeans.

"Good. Take the bus into the city tomorrow, then grab a cab. Get a room under the name Nix, make it Edward Nix, at the Waterford Hotel off Northwest Expressway. You know the place?"

"You bet."

"Stay there until you hear from me. That should be by tomorrow evening."

Rose fished through his pocket, found the keys to the Blazer and tossed them to Bolan. "You're the boss, Pollock."

2

Rush-hour traffic streamed over the cloverleaf at I-44 and Oklahoma City's Broadway Extension. Bolan closed the phone-booth door to ward off the noise and pressed the phone tighter into his ear. "Sorry, Hal," he said into the receiver. "Couldn't hear you."

"I said the guy's name is Wilson, Striker," Brognola said using Bolan's code name. "Roy Wilson. I just talked to him. Former Marine Recon. I've known him a long time."

"You trust him?"

"Implicitly. He's a good cop, and isn't afraid to bend the rules a little when it becomes necessary. Try not to run him too far out front though—he's close to a state retirement, and I'd hate to see him lose his pension." Brognola cleared his throat. When he spoke again, his voice sounded different. "I worked with Wilson several years ago on a bank-robbery-and-murder deal that went down in Tulsa. He came up with a snitch, then called us in. That would have been back . . . hell, that was just about the time I was chasing *your* butt all over the country."

Bolan chuckled. He could almost see the half-chewed stump of cigar in his old friend's mouth as the man talked, and for a moment, the "old days" returned to the Executioner's mind. After Vietnam, Bolan had declared a one-man war on the Mafia, and come close to destroying the age-old criminal organization single-handedly. But the Executioner had carried no badge, and it had taken Hal Brognola, then a young Justice Department agent himself, some time to realize that he and Bolan were on the same side.

The big Fed had led a quest to lock up the Executioner and throw away the key. But once the G-man had realized they were fighting the same war, they had joined forces. And the criminals of the world hadn't drawn an easy breath since.

"Wilson is currently in the Oklahoma State Bureau of Investigation, Special Operation Division," Brognola said, breaking into Bolan's thoughts. "Assigned to the Oil Field Theft Unit. He'll meet you at a place called Pumps on Broadway Extension in Edmond. Suburb of OKC. You know it?"

"I can find it. Anything else?"

"No. Just the usual PYA rule. Protect Your Ass, big guy."

"Always," the Executioner said and hung up.

A minute later, the warrior turned the Blazer into the traffic heading north from Oklahoma City to Edmond. He passed the usual string of grocery stores, fast-food restaurants and shopping centers, then turned into a small strip of stores and parked under an artificial gasoline tank with the nozzle affixed to the side. The Pumps, read the sign on the tank.

Roy Wilson fit Brognola's description to a T. Sitting alone at a table by the window, the OSBI undercover specialist wore a faded denim jacket, jeans, wing-tipped boots and a large silver buckle on his hand-tooled Western belt. Long hair hung over his ears and down his back, but the top of his skull shone under the overhead track lights. A small gold earring hung from his left ear, and combined with a beard that hid his throat, made him look like a cross between an Old West gunfighter and a pirate.

"Wilson?" Bolan said, taking the seat across the table.

The man nodded slowly. "And you'd be Pollock."

Bolan nodded.

"Brognola tells me you need some help," Wilson said after a brief glance around the room for curious ears. "And for Brognola, I'd do just about anything." He leaned closer. "But let me explain my situation to you. I'm two months short of retirement. And they've stuck me in the Oil Field Theft Unit—the most political unit in a political bureau in a very political state. Particularly where oil is involved. You get my drift?"

"It sounds like you don't want to risk your pension."

"That's correct. I don't *want* to."

"But you will if you have to?"

Wilson sighed, shook his head and squinted at the ceiling. Then the sigh became a chuckle. He looked back to Bolan and shook his head again. "I suppose. If that's what it takes to put the bad guys in jail. At least I always have in the past." He blew air between his closed lips and looked down at the tablecloth. "I always tell myself I won't—tell myself to play it smart and follow all the rules those pencil-neck paper-pushing geek supervisors lay down. You know, kiss ass and play the politics game? But it never seems to work out that way." He paused again. "Maybe that's why I'm not retiring any higher than Agent III after twenty years."

Bolan smiled. He liked Wilson. The guy wasn't much different than he was. He'd do what it took to get the bad guys off the streets and protect the innocent. But there was one big difference between Bolan and Wilson.

The Executioner had seen the gold wedding ring on the OSBI agent's left hand. Wilson was married, and probably had children. If so, they would be of college age now.

And that threw a whole new light on pensions and security.

A waitress wearing khaki shorts, Velcro sandals and a gray baseball jersey bearing the Pumps logo stopped at the table. Both men ordered a beer.

As soon as she'd left, Wilson said, "Brognola ran down part of the situation to me over the phone. I can see why he doesn't want to go through the usual official channels. And yeah, I'll go out on the limb for you. But I want you to realize that I'm violating about a hundred and fifty million OSBI policies by doing this without advising my inspector."

"I appreciate that," Bolan said.

"There's more you need to know. There's a lot of heat coming down in this state right now, a grand-jury investigation going on that goes all the way to the governor. Nobody's proved that he's dirty yet, but it looks like he's at least going to have to testify."

"What's it over?" Bolan asked.

"Campaign contributions, mostly. Promises of jobs for money, that sort of thing. But it ties in to other charges of kickbacks that involve the Oklahoma Corporation Commission."

"And they oversee oil production?"

"Right. One of the commissioners allegedly taped a bunch of conversations of the others talking about taking money. So I think it's safe to say somebody's dirty—either the 'taper' or the 'tapees.'"

The Executioner could see what Wilson was driving at. If Istad Itar planned to torch the oil wells of Oklahoma, there was certain intelligence information that they'd need. Like which wells were in operation. And if they wanted to do the best job possible, they'd need to know which sites had the highest production rates.

It was simple. The more oil there was at a site, the more there was to burn.

"I see where you're going," Bolan said. "and I've read between the lines. You've got your own case going parallel to the grand-jury investigation. Okay, off the record. Are the commissioners dirty?"

"Can't say about all of them. But one of them—Fred Moreland's his name—Lava soap and gasoline wouldn't wash the stink off."

"So what do you say we put this Fred Moreland in the 'trick bag'?" Bolan said.

"You've been reading my mail." Wilson grinned. "You know where to find him tonight?"

The OSBI agent's smile widened. "I know when Fred Moreland gets up in the morning, when he takes a piss and all about the little University of Oklahoma sorority girl he's putting through college in return for services rendered." Wilson looked at his watch. "And right about now, old Fred'll be having his third Singapore Sling at the Rig Club down by the state capital." He stood up. "Shall we?"

Bolan followed the man out the door to a Ford Bronco with a whip antenna. Wilson unlocked the door, and the warrior slid into the passenger seat.

"This going to bring the heat down on you at the office?" the Executioner asked.

"Only if they find out about it," Wilson said matter-of-factly as he slid behind the wheel. "But Fred Moreland damn sure deserves it."

"If he's dirty, he does."

Wilson backed out of the parking lot. "I wasn't thinking of that," he replied, turning toward Bolan. He smiled wryly. "It's those Singapore Slings he drinks. Anybody who likes those sissy-shit things deserves the death penalty."

THE OUTSIDE of the Rig Club looked like an abandoned warehouse, which was exactly what it had been until the oil boom of the seventies, when sixty-dollar-a-barrel oil prices had brought Oklahoma an unemployment rate of less than one percent, workers from all over the Western Hemisphere and a general prosperity the likes of which the state had never before experienced.

Men who had formerly been blue-collar employees went into the drilling business, or related oil-field services. New apartment buildings and motels sprang up overnight. Fifty-dollar cigars were lighted with hundred-dollar bills, Learjets were rented for overnight gambling excursions to Las Vegas, Atlantic City and the Bahamas, and champagne was consumed from thousand-dollar custom-made cowboy boots.

And the money trickled down. Off-duty highway patrolmen made two hundred dollars a night to sleep with their Mini-14s on highly productive leases. Triple salaries lured talented police detectives away from their departments and into the private theft investigation of crude oil and equipment. Patrolmen spent their off-duty hours guarding banks whose vaults held ten times the usual cash.

It had been much like the gold strikes of the nineteenth century, and there was, in general, a vulgar display of wealth. Country clubs doubled their memberships, then doubled them again and again as the money kept pouring in. Exclusive new bars—the Rig Club among the most elite—sprang up in redecorated grocery stores, warehouses, offices buildings and even deserted railroad cars.

Then, almost overnight, oil plummeted to eighteen dollars a barrel. And the nouveau riche fell with it. But the old-time oilmen, who had seen the price of oil rise and fall all their lives, and knew better than to overextend their resources, remained. They had always favored the Rig Club, and their patronage had kept the place open when most of the other new clubs fell by the wayside.

Roy Wilson had run down the situation to the Executioner on the drive over. OSBI, or simply "the bureau" as Wilson called it, had been tailing Moreland for nearly two months. The drive from Edmond had also provided an opportunity for the two men to work out a cursory plan to "introduce" the warrior to the commissioner.

The Bronco pulled to a halt in the parking lot amid a curious mixture of Mercedes, Lincolns, Cadillacs and pickup trucks. Wilson opened the Rig's front door and stepped back.

Bolan glanced down at his jeans and boots. "You sure we're dressed all right?" he asked. Looking out of place during an undercover mission of this nature would only draw attention.

Wilson laughed softly. "This is Oklahoma, boy," he said, exaggerating his accent into a twanging nasal drawl. "You wear a necktie through this door, they'll lynch you with it."

The warrior stepped inside and stopped, letting his eyes adjust to the darkness. As his pupils dilated, he saw that the OSBI agent had exaggerated somewhat. The fact was, all manner of dress appeared appropriate inside the club, and the Executioner saw business suits and ties mixing in with the jeans and boots. Two couples at a table against the wall even wore formal evening dress, and as he passed on his way to the ornately carved bar at the rear of the room, he heard a woman in a sequined gown talking excitedly about the *Will Rogers Follies*.

Wilson moved in next to Bolan at the bar. "Got your story down?"

Bolan nodded. "You looked around? Anybody know you?"

"Oh, yeah," Wilson said. He turned around and rested his back against the bar. "The two guys in the corner," he whispered out of the corner of his mouth. "But they don't want to be ID'd any more than we do. OBNDD—Oklahoma Bureau of Narcotics and Dangerous Drugs."

The Executioner followed the agent's glance toward a table where a man wearing a tan Western-cut suit sat talking to a woman in tight designer jeans and boots. He felt a presence behind him, and turned to see that the bartender had appeared.

"Coors," Wilson told the man.

Bolan nodded.

The bartender placed two frosty mugs on the counter and turned to the sink. Wilson took a sip.

"Which one's Moreland?" the Executioner whispered.

The agent's eyes flashed to the center of the room where a white-haired man in a conservative blue suit looked as if he were holding court. Younger men circled the table. Dressed identically to the commissioner, they leaned toward the older man, hanging on to every word that came out of his wrinkled lips.

"Good thing it ain't winter," Wilson commented. "Their lips would be froze solid to old Fred's ass."

Bolan smiled. "You ready?"

Wilson nodded. His hand rose to his beard, and he rubbed his chin. "Go as easy as you can. I don't heal as quick as when I was younger." Lifting his beer, he started across the bar toward the men's room. Two steps from Fred Moreland's table, the toe of one of his wing-tipped boots caught the rug and he went stumbling toward the commissioner.

Beer flew from the mug, showering Moreland.

Wilson caught his fall on the edge of the table. "Sorry, old padnuh," he slurred drunkenly. Pushing away from the table, he started to step away.

Moreland reached up and caught his arm. "You stupid drunken pig," he snapped, his dark eyes flashing in anger.

Wilson stopped. Swaying slightly, he said, "Hey, old man. I said I was sorry. Now fuck off."

Moreland's eyes opened wide in astonishment. "Do you know who you're talking to?" he demanded.

The Executioner had been inching his way toward the table. He had seen the frightened faces of the younger men around the table. They could see that violence, something they were hardly accustomed to, was a real possibility within the next few seconds. So what were they supposed to do? Stand up to this drunken cowboy to impress their boss and get stomped into the floor of the Rig Club? Or stay out of it, and send their careers into a sudden nosedive?

Bolan solved their dilemma for them.

Wilson took a sip of the beer remaining in his mug, then spit it into Moreland's face. As the commissioner sputtered in shock, the OSBI agent drew back a fist.

The Executioner caught Wilson's arm from behind as the punch started toward the commissioner's head. Spinning the agent around, he said, "Hey, Jesse, settle down."

Wilson's other arm drew back, the heavy glass beer mug clenched in his fingers. As it started forward, Bolan sent a hard right cross into his chin.

The agent slumped forward into Bolan's arms. "Son of a bitch," he whispered into the Executioner's ear. "That your idea of going easy?"

Bolan didn't answer. He hoisted Wilson over his shoulder, then looked at Moreland. "Sorry. Guy gets a little rowdy when he drinks." Without further words, he started toward the door.

"Wow," one of the younger men at the table said, "did you see that?"

In case anyone had followed and was watching through the door, Bolan carried the OSBI agent all the way to the Bronco, opening the door, then laid him in across the seat. "You okay?" he asked as Wilson opened his eyes.

"I'll live." The agent grinned, rubbing his chin again. "But just barely. Go get 'em, hoss."

The Executioner returned to the Rig Club, stopped at the bar and ordered another beer.

"It's paid for," the bartender said as he set it in front of Bolan. "By Mr. Moreland."

The warrior turned toward the table, held up the mug and nodded his thanks.

A moment later, one of the younger men was crossing the room. "Mr. Moreland would like to thank you personally," he said.

Bolan shook his head and smiled. "It's not necessary."

"Oh, yes, it is." The man's eyeglasses fell down the bridge of his nose and he pushed them back up.

"When Mr. Moreland wants something, it's *very* necessary."

The warrior shrugged and followed the man to the table.

Thanks to a fistful of napkins and the handkerchiefs of the sycophants circling the table, Fred Moreland was almost dry by the time he waved Bolan into the chair vacated by his messenger. "You have my personal thanks," he said in a tone of voice that sounded like a king bestowing knighthood. "Please, sit down."

Bolan nodded and dropped into the chair.

"I'm Fred Moreland. And you are..."

"Fraser," Bolan replied. "James. But call me Blackie. Most people do."

Moreland smiled. "What a colorful nickname. How did you receive it?"

Bolan chuckled. "It's a long story. No point in boring you with it."

"Someday you must."

"Sure. But first, let me tell you that I think it's me who should be apologizing to you. Jesse—" he nodded toward the door "—works for me. He's a good man usually. Just gets a little wild after a couple of beers."

"And what kind of work do you two do?"

"Security. Corporate, mainly. But I'm looking into the feasibility of an oil-field branch in Texas and Oklahoma."

Moreland's eyes flashed suddenly with interest. Behind the interest, Bolan could see the greed. "There isn't as much theft as there was when prices were high," the commissioner said. He smiled. "The joke is, that if you're not careful these days, someone will dump a load of crude into your tank."

The young men around the table hooted with false laughter.

"But seriously," Moreland went on. "There is still a good deal of money to be made in the 'patch,' as some so rudely call it." He turned to the men around the table. "Gentlemen, perhaps you should be attending to other business?"

Moreland's entourage rose as one and left the table.

"Tell me, Mr. Fraser... or Blackie, if you will. Exactly what did you have in mind?"

Bolan shrugged. "High-tech stuff, primarily. Electronic surveillance. I figure I can outfit leases with hidden cameras, alarms, that sort of thing. Use a roving patrol with sensors. Five men will be able to secure as many leases as fifty did in the past."

Moreland's eyebrows lowered. "I would think there might be quite a temptation for the guards to do their own stealing under the circumstances."

Bolan allowed a tiny smile to flash on his face, then went deadpan. "I'm sure the temptation would be there."

The commissioner had thrown out the bait. Satisfied now that it had been struck, he shifted gears. "Tell me," he said. "How is your feasibility study going? Are you encountering any problems?"

"The answers are well, and yes. I'm convinced the business would work. But I'm having a problem making contacts. This is a pretty closed society down here.''

Moreland chuckled. ''We Okies tend to be as bad as New Englanders in that respect. Perhaps I could be of some assistance. I do command some small amount of influence.'' His smile made sure the Executioner knew he was being overly modest.

''That would definitely help, Mr. Moreland,'' Bolan said. ''Exactly what did you have in mind?''

''Oh, a partnership of sorts. In your business, it never hurts to know someone in mine.'' The commissioner reached into his coat pocket and dropped an embossed business card on the table. ''Why don't you stop by my office in the morning? We could discuss it further.'' He paused. ''There is still a great deal of money to be made in crude-oil production, Blackie,'' he said. ''It just works a little differently than it did during the boom.''

''How's that?''

''During the boom, we produced oil and then sold it,'' Moreland said.

''And now?''

''Now we have to steal it and sell it.''

3

By 7:45 a.m. Lincoln Boulevard was alive with state employees scurrying toward their offices in the capital area. Bolan guided the Blazer through the sea of vehicles toward the ancient stone edifice in the distance. Distinctive for its lack of a dome, the Oklahoma State Capital Building had another characteristic equally uncommon.

It was the only such structure among the fifty states that had a producing oil well on the grounds.

The Executioner passed the bobbing pump jack, then the building itself, and turned toward a smaller structure. He had traded his jeans and shirt for a beige two-piece suit, off-white oxford shirt and conservative brown tie. The clothes weren't only more suitable for a visit to the capital area, it afforded concealment for his weapons. The Beretta now rode under his arm in a leather shoulder holster. The larger, and far more powerful Magnum .44 Desert Eagle had been strapped to his right hip under the jacket. In addition to the guns, the Executioner carried a Cold Steel Mini-Tanto in a leather sheath at the small of his back.

In the true tradition of Southwest businessmen and politicians, however, Bolan had retained the bumpy ostrich boots. Oklahomans, Bolan knew, were fiercely proud of their pioneer heritage, and while they might concede to wearing suits tailored on the "wrong side of the Mississippi," their footwear would be coming from no farther than San Antonio.

Rain clouds had gathered by the time the Executioner pulled into an empty spot in the parking lot of the Jim Thorpe building. An attractive woman in a black Nissan pulled in next to him as he got out. Wearing a conservative black business suit, she followed him toward a side door in the concrete.

As he held the door for the woman, the Executioner noticed several men, suspended on rope platforms, washing the upper windows of the building. He followed her down the hall toward the elevators, passing a number of photographs and paintings of Jim Thorpe, the great Native American athlete for whom the building had been named.

The woman leaned forward, pushed the up button, then stared silently ahead at the gray doors.

Bolan followed her into the car, noticing several streaks of gray in her hair. Rather than detract from her looks, they enhanced them, emphasizing a beauty found only in women who have lived, seen and experienced the world.

The elevator stopped on the second floor. Bolan stepped out as a man holding a foam coffee cup took his place in the car. "Good morning, Paula," the man said as the doors closed.

The Executioner glanced at the first office on his right as he made his way down the hall. T. J. Lott, the frosted glass door read, Oklahoma Corporation

Commissioner. Bolan vaguely remembered Lott as once being a highly respected running back for the University of Oklahoma football team.

The warrior's feet sank into plush carpet as he pushed through the door to Fred Moreland's reception area. A tall, painfully thin middle-aged woman sat behind the desk facing the door. Her hair had been cropped nearly as short as the Executioner's, and her gaunt lips barely moved as she spoke into the phone against her ear. She glanced up as Bolan came to a halt in front of her desk, said, "Be with you in a moment," then went back to whispering into the receiver.

When she hung up, Bolan said, "Good morning. Mr. Fraser to see Commissioner Moreland."

The woman's gaze dropped to a notepad by the phone. She smiled coldly, revealing a row of perfectly capped teeth that were by far her best feature. "Please have a seat, Mr. Fraser. Commissioner Moreland will be with you shortly."

Bolan sat on a couch along the wall. He had gone to the trouble he had last night to assure himself that Fred Moreland was indeed as dirty as Roy Wilson suspected. As always, he had found playing the role of an equally dishonest man distasteful. It had, however, been a necessary evil.

But the time for that necessary evil was almost over.

The phone buzzed on the receptionist's desk. "Mr. Fraser is here," the woman said. "Yes..." She glanced up at the Executioner. "Yes, sir. I'll send him in." She nodded to Bolan.

He stood and walked past the woman as she opened a door to the side of her desk. A second later, Moreland was rising and circling the stacks of papers and files on his own desk.

The Executioner was surprised at the financially conservative decor of the room. He had pegged Moreland for a "high roller" last night, but the budget furniture that now met his eyes seemed to contradict that deduction.

The commissioner hurried forward, grasped the Executioner's hand, then motioned him toward a sitting area away from the desk. "Have a seat, Mr. Fraser, er, Blackie. And please excuse the modest embellishments." The grin that spread across his face was just short of a leer. "Wouldn't do to make the taxpayers think their money was being wasted on such frivolous things as chairs, though, would it?" He winked at Bolan as he took a seat in a worn armchair.

Bolan sat across from him.

"I'm afraid I'm a little pressed for time this morning," Moreland said, glancing at his watch. "Meeting the governor later. This grand-jury nonsense, and all. And I have a few odds and ends to take care of ahead of time. So if you don't mind, I'll get straight to the point." He crossed his legs. "From what you told me last night, I believe you and I can do business. You get set up with your electronics, and keep your personnel to a skeleton crew. Men that know oil and know equipment. And above all, men you can trust not to get a bellyful of beer—like that man last night—and open their mouths to the wrong people." His voice rose slightly with excitement. "We can bleed crude off the tanks under your control several times a week. I already have arrangements with saltwater disposal and reclaiming plants. They'll buy it from us. Now equipment—valves, jacks, drill bits, that sort of thing—that's a bit trickier. Easier to trace, and we'll have to be more careful. But it can be done. The bottom line is, if you steal it, I can find a place to sell it."

Bolan forced a smile. "What's your cut?"

"Half," Moreland said without hesitation. "For that you get the security that even if one of your men gets caught, we can cover it somewhere along the way." He straightened his tie, then smoothed the lapels of his jacket. "Believe me, Blackie, we've got a gold mine here. A *black gold* mine."

Bolan heard a scratching sound behind him. Glancing over his shoulder, he saw a dark-complected window washer being lowered on a rope platform. The man held a squeegee in one hand. A bucket rested on the wood at his feet.

The Executioner turned back. He needed privacy for his interrogation. But his back was to the window, and the window washer wouldn't notice what was happening if he kept his hands in front of him.

"Well, what do you say?" Moreland asked.

The warrior reached inside his jacket, his fingers wrapping around the grips of the big Desert Eagle in the holster on his hip. As he drew the weapon from leather, he said, "I say that the rules of the game have just changed."

Suddenly Fred Moreland was looking down a .44-caliber bore. The smile fell from his face like a dead leaf from a tree, and the color drained from his cheeks.

"I want my attorney," he said weakly.

Careful to keep the Desert Eagle in front of his body and out of view from the window, Bolan said, "Wrong game."

"But...but..." Moreland sputtered. "I have rights." Then, coming out of his initial shock at the sight of the gun, the color began to return to his face. "Are you OSBI or federal?" he snarled. "Not that it matters. I'll have whatever badge it is you're carrying over this." He started to stand. "I have the right to a—"

Bolan leaned forward, crumpled a handful of the man's lapel in his fist and pushed him back down into the chair. "You only have two rights at the moment. The right to answer the questions I'm about to ask you. Give up that right, and the only right you'll have left is the right to die."

Moreland's mouth fell open as the blood left his face once again.

"Somewhere in the recent past, you sold information to somebody concerning oil production statistics. I want to know who you sold that information to."

Moreland continued to stare. "You aren't a police officer of some kind?" he asked. "Then who—"

Bolan cocked the hammer of the Desert Eagle and the sound echoed through the silent room. "The man who's going to kill you if you don't give me what I want. Don't forget your rights. You're getting dangerously close to experiencing the second one."

Moreland's eyebrows lowered in nervous concentration. "A week or so ago a man approached me. A foreigner. They were setting up a new drilling company—"

"What was the name of the company?" Bolan demanded.

Moreland closed his eyes, squinting hard. "Wind... Windsong? No, Windfield Exploration. That was it. The Arabs often use American names to avoid prejudice."

"Do you have any idea why they wanted the information?"

"Isn't it obvious?" Moreland said. "Oil is found in underground lakes. If they find out that a certain site another company leases is producing a hundred barrels a day, they can buy up the leases around it."

"I want the same list," Bolan said.

The commissioner looked down the barrel of the big Desert Eagle, then spun to the filing cabinet behind his desk. He reached into his pocket.

"Careful," the Executioner warned.

Moreland pulled a key out of his pants and inserted it into the filing cabinet. A second later, he turned back to face Bolan. "This is—"

The man never got a chance to say another word.

Bolan heard the sound of cracking glass, and a third eye suddenly appeared in Fred Moreland's forehead. Unlike the other two, this one bubbled a red froth. The man's face froze, both of his real eyes staring at Bolan with a dull cloudiness covering the pupils. The file fell from his hand to the desk in front of him.

The Executioner dived to the floor as more rounds ripped into his chair. The wooden platform disappeared above the window, and he rose to his feet, racing forward. Grasping the wooden frame atop the glass, the warrior pulled up.

The window didn't budge; the frame had been painted shut. Drawing the Mini-Tanto knife from the sheath on his belt, he sliced along the sides of the glass, then across the sill. A moment later the wood creaked as he shoved it up.

The big .44 leading the way, Bolan stuck his head out the window to see that the washing platform had stopped on the floor directly above Moreland's office. The man in the striped overalls—the Executioner could see now he was of Middle Eastern descent—was preparing to enter the window of an office one space over. He still held the squeegee in one hand.

In the other was a 9 mm pistol with a sound suppressor threaded onto the barrel.

Bolan aimed up at the man's chest. "Freeze!" he ordered. A dead body would do him no good. He needed the man alive.

The assassin looked down, saw the gun and did as ordered. Both the squeegee and the gun fell from his hands, dropping past Bolan to clatter against the sidewalk below.

Fear flickered across the window washer's face. He glanced to the window, then back at Bolan. A moment later, the man dived into the opening.

The Executioner cursed under his breath and turned toward the door, holstering the Desert Eagle. The shot through the window would have been inaudible in the reception area. Unless he missed his guess, the emaciated woman behind the desk would have no idea what had transpired. He hoped so. He needed to find the man in the overalls. That task would be complicated beyond all possibility of success if he had to dodge the police at the same time.

As he opened the door and stepped into the reception area, the woman looked up from her novel.

"Commissioner Moreland asked me to tell you that he doesn't want to be disturbed," the warrior said as he walked briskly toward the hall.

The woman shrugged and went back to her book.

As soon as he was in the hall, Bolan broke into a sprint. He pushed through the door to the stairs and took them three at a time to the floor above, drawing the big .44 Magnum as he reached the landing.

The hallway was deserted as he stepped out of the stairwell. Hurrying toward the office that the Arab had dived into, Bolan rounded a corner just in time to see a pair of legs, clad in striped overalls dart into a side hall.

The warrior raced forward. The assassin heard his footsteps, turned, then sprinted down the hall. The Executioner pursued, gaining a half step on the man with each three they took down the long corridor.

The Arab slowed slightly and stuck his hand into the bib of his overalls.

The Executioner knew that the Arab was trying to draw his backup gun. If he did, Bolan would have no choice but to shoot.

And if he killed the man, he lost a source of information about Istad Itar.

Still ten yards behind the Arab, Bolan heard an office door open. He left his feet as the assassin's hand came out of the overalls holding a snub-nosed revolver.

The man started to turn. As he did, a woman stepped out of the open door into the hall.

Bolan hit her in midair, knocking her forward into the gunner. "You stupid son of a—" the woman shouted as all three of them landed in a heap on the hallway carpet.

Bolan spun out of the mess to the side and leaped to his feet, bringing up the Desert Eagle in a two-handed grip. Five feet away, the man in the overalls had his arm wrapped around the woman in the black suit who had parked next to the warrior in the parking lot, then accompanied him into the building.

The stubby barrel of the revolver pressed into her temple.

"Drop the gun!" the Arab screamed in heavily accented English. "I will kill her!"

Bolan looked toward the woman. *Paula.* That was what the man in the elevator had called her.

The Executioner was surprised to see no fear in the woman's eyes. Concern, yes—this could hardly be an everyday occurrence for her. But she showed no signs of panic. Their eyes met.

Paula's teeth were clamped in restrained anger. "Would you please shoot this son of a bitch for me?" she said.

"Shut up!" the assassin shouted, tightening his grip. "I will kill you!"

Bolan shifted the Desert Eagle slightly, trying to let the sights fall on the small patch of face behind the woman's shoulder. The man in the overalls dropped lower behind his hostage, using the woman's body as a shield.

"Drop it! Drop it! I will not tell you again," the Arab ordered.

Bolan stared into the woman's eyes, trying to will the message to her. *Move. It doesn't matter which way. Just move enough to give me a target for one split second.*

Paula seemed to understand. Ever so slightly, she nodded her head and took a deep breath.

A moment later, the woman twisted violently to the side, bringing her arm up and sweeping the gun from the side of her head.

The Arab screamed his rage and pulled the trigger.

The snub-nose exploded, the round missing the woman's head by an inch, driving into the wall of the hallway.

Still in the headlock, Paula dropped low as the gun swung back toward her head.

Bolan fired.

The .44 Magnum hollowpoint drilled out of the barrel and into the Arab's face, driving him backward. His arm froze in death around the woman's neck, dragging her to the floor on top of him.

The Executioner raced forward as the woman jerked free of the arm and rose to her feet. She looked down at the man on the floor for a moment. Then, slowly and deliberately, she brought her leg back and kicked him solidly in the ribs.

Bolan glanced at the assassin. The top half of his head had been blown away. "It's all right," he said.

"Like hell it is. Shoot him again. Make *sure* he's dead."

Doors began to open up and down the hall. Heads began to peek out. "What's happening?" an unknown voice asked.

Bolan knew that in seconds the floor would be crawling with cops. It was time to go.

Still staring down at the body, Paula extended her hand toward the Executioner. "If you don't want to shoot him again, give me your gun and *I'll* shoot him."

When she got no answer, the woman turned toward the big man at her side.

And found herself alone in the hall.

4

Roy Wilson looked as if fire might come shooting out of his nostrils as Bolan stepped into room 14 at the Holiday Inn on I-40. He rose from his chair at the table, pulled the denim jacket off his back and slammed it onto the bed. "You have any idea what kind of position you've just put me in?" he asked.

Bolan nodded. A bad one. He understood that, could appreciate it and was sorry it had happened. But it couldn't be helped.

"I'm harboring a fucking fugitive," Wilson said. "They think you killed Fred Moreland."

The warrior nodded again, taking a seat across from Wilson and indicating with a sweep of the hand that the OSBI agent should sit down.

The Executioner had called Brognola immediately after leaving the capital area, giving the Justice man a quick rundown of his progress and requesting that the big Fed call Wilson at the hotel and inform the agent of what had occurred. His mission at the Oklahoma Corporation Commission wasn't complete yet, and he needed Wilson's continued help.

Wilson sat back down, shaking his head. Bolan didn't speak. The man needed a few seconds to sort things out, and the Executioner owed him that much. Finally the agent ran a hand over his balding pate and looked up. "Okay, this one's for Brognola. Maybe *he* can give me a job when they fire me and take away my pension. That is, if I'm not in the damn penitentiary by then."

Bolan smiled. "You won't be."

"Yeah, right. Easy for you to say." He ran his hand back over his head, took a deep breath and continued. "Okay, Pollock. Tell me what happened, and what you still need."

The Executioner explained what had gone down and what he had learned about Windfield Exploration. "It's a front for Istad Itar. I'm convinced of it. Moreland thought he was selling info to Arabs intent on eliminating the competition. Well, he was right to a certain degree. They want to eliminate the high-production wells, all right."

"But not for business reasons," Wilson finished for him. "They want to burn them."

Bolan nodded. "What I need is the same list of wells that Moreland sold the terrorists. A few more minutes, and I'd have had it."

"Why did they kill Moreland?" Wilson asked.

"They didn't need him anymore, and they didn't want to take any chances that he'd talk."

"So, how do you plan to get the list?" the agent asked. "Moreland's office is going to be crawling with Capital Police officers. And some of the guys from the bureau are on their way out there right now."

"I need an inside man," the Executioner said. "Or maybe I should say a woman."

Wilson had been staring at the table. Now he looked up. "You mean the woman in the hall?"

"Right. She's tough. I think if I leveled with her, she might help."

Wilson snorted. "Maybe. But we don't even know who she is. What did she look like?"

"Very attractive," Bolan said. "Tall, maybe five-eight. Brown hair with gray streaks. I'd say in her early forties."

"That could fit a lot of women."

"Yes, it could." The warrior pulled a scrap of paper out of his pocket. "But this won't. I got her license number as I left."

Wilson took the scrap of paper, stood and walked to the phone on the desk. A moment later, he had the Oklahoma Department of Public Safety on the line. He read the plate number, gave them the number of the hotel, then hung up. He returned to his chair.

"How long will this take?" Bolan asked. "We need to get rolling. If I'm wrong and this Paula lady won't help, we need to figure out another—"

"What did you say?"

"I said if she won't help, we need to find another plan of attack."

"No, you mentioned her name. You know her name?"

"First only. Guy on the elevator called her Paula."

A slow smile etched its way through Wilson's beard, curling his mustache. He repeated Bolan's description of the woman. "Tall, good-looking, early forties. Brown hair and a few gray streaks?"

Bolan nodded.

"And it looked like she worked there in the Jim Thorpe building?"

"Yeah."

Wilson stood and pulled his jean jacket from the bed. "We don't need to wait for the DPS," he said. "I know her."

Bolan rose and followed him toward the door. "You think she'll be willing to help?"

The agent twisted the knob and pulled the door halfway open. "Pollock," he said, turning back to the Executioner, "you'd have to know her like I do to appreciate this, but I don't think she'd miss it for the world."

THE KIETHLEY SCHOOL of Martial Arts was across from the state fairgrounds, squeezed between a craft store and a florist shop in a small shopping strip. *Karate, Judo, and Aikido* had been painted in red across the top of the large picture window set in the gray concrete front. Photographs of men and women in the white pajamalike uniforms known as *gis* had been taped to the glass. Beyond them, Bolan could see a large shelf of trophies running along the side wall.

A late-morning class—primarily housewives and retirees—was in progress on the tiled floor. It was being conducted by a young woman wearing a black belt.

Bolan watched Wilson exit the door, walk across the street and slide back behind the wheel of the Bronco. "Gal teaching the class just talked to Jack," he said. "He went to pick up Paula, and they should be here in a few minutes."

The warrior nodded. He and Wilson had returned to the Jim Thorpe building to find the parking lot crowded with police and press vehicles. Bolan, who could be identified, remained in the car while the agent checked on the situation.

Jack Kiethley had joined his wife at the Jim Thorpe building as Oklahoma City police and OSBI agents had concluded their interviews with Paula. Wilson had overheard Kiethley trying to talk his wife into taking the rest of the day off.

"You sure she won't just go back to work?" Bolan asked as they stared at the karate school.

Wilson smiled. "It's possible, but I don't think so. Those two have been good friends of mine for years. Even Paula will be a little shaken up after all that's happened. She won't admit it bothered her, and she'll argue with Jack long enough to make it look like it was *her* idea to take off. But then she'll do it."

"Tell me about them," Bolan said. "I need to know what we're getting into."

"Jack used to be with OSBI. Special agent, and our top unarmed-combat instructor. He quit several years ago."

"Why?" Bolan asked.

Wilson chuckled. "Some men just aren't cut out for bureaucracy. Need to be on their own. The words 'Jack Kiethley' and 'insubordination' were becoming synonymous around the bureau by the time he pulled out and opened up this place."

"Is he going to be a problem?" The last thing Bolan needed for what he was planning was a man who couldn't take orders.

"Not if he respects you. And oh, he'll *love* you. But he drove the supervisors absolutely nuts. Especially the wimps who did nothing but push paper." He frowned in concentration. "What was it Jack used to call them? Oh, yeah. 'Bureaucratic pencil-necked ass-kissing sycophants.' You know the type?"

Bolan nodded. He had known his share.

"Anyway, you convince Jack Kiethley that he can trust you and you're his friend, he'll follow you through the gates of hell. But if he gets the impression you're lying to him, or trying to use him, forget it." Wilson paused. "And I pity the poor fool who tries to take advantage of Paula if Jack gets his hands on him. He loves that woman like you wouldn't believe."

Bolan thought back to Paula's cool behavior both before and after he'd shot the man taking her hostage. "I think I'd pity the poor fool Paula got her hands on."

Wilson laughed. "Good point."

A red Suzuki Sidekick 4X4 pulled into a reserved parking place in front of the building. Bolan watched a stocky bearded man about five-ten get out.

A white Dodge pulled in next to it. The driver's-side window came down as the man walked toward it.

Wilson and Bolan stepped out of the Bronco and walked across the street toward the two vehicles.

Jack Kiethley wore faded blue jeans, a cutoff sweatshirt and lightweight black-and-white martial-arts shoes. He noticed the two men coming toward him as he stopped at the Dodge's window. His hand moved quickly under his shirt, but it fell back as he recognized Roy Wilson.

Wilson glanced at Bolan and laughed. "Now I wonder what could be under that raggedy-ass sweatshirt?" he said loud enough for Kiethley to hear.

Turning back to the man, he said, "You got a concealed carry license, old buddy?"

Kiethley laughed. "Oklahoma law makes no such provisions. But I couldn't expect some cretin OSBI agent to know that." He paused long enough to help his wife out of the car. "I thought we'd seen the last of you state incompetents for one day."

"Who'd they send over?"

"Wilfred and Duffy," Kiethley replied, shaking his head. "Director must have known I was involved and done it just to spite me." He was still smiling, but now the smile began to fade. "This a social call or more about... *that?*"

"More about that. Sort of."

Kiethley turned to Bolan, his face tightening as he studied the face. It was obvious that he had heard a description of the man suspected in Moreland's murder, and had just realized he was looking at him.

"This is Rance Pollock," Wilson said. "And no, he didn't kill Moreland. But we need to talk to you." He glanced at Kiethley's wife. "Both of you."

The former agent took his wife's arm. "Let's go in."

Bolan and Wilson followed the two into a small room just inside the front door. They removed their shoes, then proceeded across the tile to an office area at the rear of the building. Kiethley pulled up his shirt, jerked a stainless-steel Colt Commander .45 from the waistband of his jeans and dropped it on his desk.

"Naughty, naughty," Wilson chided. "You're a civilian now, you know."

Kiethley snorted and pulled the desk chair around to face a couch along the wall.

"Jack," Wilson said, dropping down between Paula and Bolan on the couch. "We need both of your help. But before we run things down to you, we want your promise of secrecy—even if you turn us down."

Jack Kiethley nodded. "There aren't too many folks where you work who'd get the time of day out of me, Roy. In fact you and the deputy director might be the only ones."

Wilson turned to Paula, who nodded.

"Pollock?" Wilson said.

Bolan studied both faces for a moment. His gut instincts told him he was looking at two people who still considered their word to be sacred, a man and a woman who could be trusted to do business with a handshake. He proceeded to explain the bare bones of the mission.

When he'd finished, and told the Kiethleys what he still needed and what he had planned, the former OSBI agent sat silently for a moment. "You realize what could happen to my wife if we get caught?"

Bolan nodded. "My man in Washington will pull all the strings he can. But I can't promise anything."

"We could all end up in prison," Kiethley said. "Not to mention the fact that Paula's pension with the Department of Community Planning is the only one we have left."

"I won't lie to you," Bolan replied. "Getting caught is a distinct possibility."

Kiethley leaned forward and rested his elbows on his knees. Making a tent out of the fingers of both hands, he placed his chin on them and closed his eyes.

Bolan waited. Like Wilson, Kiethley needed some time to sort things out. But the warrior had no doubt about the conclusion to which the man would come. Cops were like soldiers in their order of loyalty. Their partners came first, then their departments, and then whatever organization that department represented. Wilson was risking his butt because of his loyalty to Hal Brognola. The Executioner had no doubt that Kiethley would do the same for Roy Wilson.

Kiethley's eyes finally opened. "Okay. I'll help. But Paula's out of it."

Bolan shook his head. "It won't work."

Paula stood, smoothed her skirt and smiled at her husband. "With all due respect, honey, you aren't really the one they need. I am."

Bolan watched for Kiethley's reaction out of the corner of his eye. He needed the woman, but he didn't want to be responsible for marital problems, either.

Kiethley surprised him. "You want to do it?" he asked, turning toward his wife.

Paula shook her head. "No, I don't *want* to do it. But I think I have to."

The karate instructor nodded, then shrugged. "I learned better than to waste time arguing with you years ago."

Then, shifting his gaze toward Wilson, he said, "Roy, you and I've been through a lot. You're like a brother to me."

He turned toward Bolan. "I don't know you, Pollock, but I'm a pretty good judge of character. And I trust you." He paused. "But it's only fair to tell you, if anything happens to this woman, I plan to dedicate the rest of my life to killing you both."

Bolan nodded. In all honesty, he couldn't blame the man. But there was more at stake here than pensions, jobs, and even potential penitentiary time. Billions of dollars would go up in oil-base smoke if the four of them weren't successful in the next phase of the mission. But even that was not the real point. The lives of dozens, if not hundreds, of oil-field workers would be lost in the explosions. More men would die trying to put out the fires once they were burning.

The Executioner couldn't allow that, and he could see that the Kiethleys didn't intend to, either. He stood. "Then let's get started. The sooner we move, the better chance we have to make this work."

HOT DUST FILLED the Executioner's nostrils as he dragged himself over the rafters in the crawl space between the third and fourth floors of the Jim Thorpe building. Below, beneath the acoustical ceiling tiles, he could hear the voices of the Capital Police officers who had sealed the area around Fred Moreland's office.

Paula Kiethley, grateful for his help during her moments as a hostage, had told the cops to get lost when they demanded a description. But Moreland's secretary had practically painted a portrait. The false beard, white overalls and paint buckets he had carried had gotten him into the building. But they would go only so far, Bolan knew. The Capital cops and OSBI agents were no fools, and if any of them took the time to look at him closely, he'd be made.

The Executioner moved to a spot just in front of the elevator shaft and waited as the car rose. The bell chimed, the doors opened and he heard Roy Wilson's voice as he crept down the top of the hall.

No, he couldn't get too close to the action. But he had no intentions of staying away and leaving Wilson or Jack and Paula Kiethley holding the bag if his plan blew up in their faces. If worse came to worst, he could always drop from the ceiling and distract the policemen long enough to allow Jack and Paula to get the Windfield file from the top of Moreland's desk. Once they had possession of that, if they were caught, there would be nothing the Executioner or anyone else could do for them.

Bolan heard the footsteps beneath him halt. Slowly he inched one of the ceiling tiles aside and peered down.

Below he could see the top of the head of a uniformed man holding a walkie-talkie. The Capital policeman stood blocking the hall that led to Moreland's office. Roy Wilson's wing-tipped cowboy boots stepped into view. Just behind him, Bolan could see the feet of Jack and Paula Kiethley. "OSBI," Wilson said, holding up a credential case.

The Capital cop shook his head. "Sorry. Agents Wilfred and Duffy are already inside. They said not to let anybody else in."

Wilson let out a deep breath. "Go ask them. But first, who's your shift captain?"

"Huh? Uh, Captain McIntire."

"Okay, go ask Wilfred and Duffy. In the meantime, I'll give Charlie a call."

The cop gulped. "You know the captain?"

"Oh, yeah," Wilson smiled.

The officer spun on his heel and hurried down the hall. Bolan maneuvered over the rafters again, coming to a halt above the office where he had sat with Fred Moreland a few hours earlier. Silently he shifted another of the tiles.

Directly below, he saw the door leading from Moreland's office to the reception area. Dropping down on his belly, he angled toward the desk.

Moreland's body had been taken away. Two men in business suits occupied the room. One, of medium height and frail build, stood holding a notepad and pen. The other, broad, bulky and looking for all the world like a college defensive tackle in stance, was on his hands and knees on the carpet.

The file containing the list of producing wells sat where it had fallen atop the pile of paperwork on Moreland's desk. So far, the two OSBI agents hadn't gotten around to checking it.

The uniformed man appeared at the door and cleared his throat.

"What is it?" the big tackle asked, turning toward the door irritably.

"Er, there's an Agent Wilson outside wanting to get in."

The frail man answered. "Get rid of him."

"But—"

"Just do it," the tackle grunted.

The cop nodded and turned away.

The warrior retraced his steps, crawling back to the place where the Kiethleys stood. Wilson had rejoined them.

"I'm sorry," he heard the cop say. "But—" The crackling of his walkie-talkie interrupted him.

"Capital dispatch to Unit 427. Come in 427."

The cop held the radio to his lips. "427 here. Go ahead."

A gruff voice replaced the feminine one that had initiated the radio transmission. "Holderman, is that you?"

"Yes, sir, Captain McIntire."

"Roy Wilson with you?"

"Affirmative."

"You got some problem? He wants in, you let him in."

"Yes, sir."

A moment later, Roy Wilson walked past the cop. When Jack and Paula Kiethley tried to follow, Holderman stepped in their way. "I'm sorry. He didn't say anything about anyone else."

Wilson turned and looked up at the taller uniformed man. Bolan saw the cold icy stare in the agent's pale blue eyes.

"I'm sick of playing games with you, pal. These two are with *me*. Now get the hell out of their way, or Charlie McIntire will be the least of your problems."

The cop did as ordered.

Bolan followed them above the ceiling, stopping once more at the tile he'd shifted over Moreland's office.

The bulky man jumped to his feet as Wilson strode into the room. "I told Holderman—"

"Simmer down, Duffy," Wilson said.

The frail man stiffened as Jack Kiethley followed his wife into the office. "What's *he* doing here?"

Kiethley smiled. "You probably hadn't heard, Wilfred. I'm back as the new director. Get ready to clean out your desk."

The two OSBI agents' faces went white for a moment. Then Wilfred saw through the lie and said, "Bullshit."

"Damn, nothing slips by you, does it?" Kiethley smiled. "In case you hadn't heard, my wife got attacked in this building this morning. And while she'd have no trouble kicking the shit out of guys like you and Duffy there, I came along just in case we ran into any real men."

Bolan smiled. There was obviously no love lost between the two agents below and their former colleague.

"Okay, okay, time out!" Wilson held up a hand. "Paula lost an earring somewhere up here this morning and she's come back to find it."

"An earring?" Wilfred repeated incredulously. "You want to ruin the investigation of an Oklahoma

Corporation Commissioner's murder over a fuckin' *earring?*"

"We aren't here to ruin anything," Wilson said. "It belonged to her grandmother is all, and she wants it back."

Bolan noticed Jack Kiethley angling away from Wilson. "You should understand about earrings, Wilfred," he said. "Don't you wear one? In your *right* ear, I hear, when you hang out with your boyfriends down at the Saddle Sore Inn."

Wilson was almost behind the two men now. Close to the desk, but still not within reach of the file. Duffy glanced over his shoulder, but turned back to Kiethley as the martial-arts instructor said, "Or are you and Duffy going steady now?"

"All right, get out!" Wilfred screamed.

Paula came to the rescue. "I'll only be a second." Dropping quickly to her hands and knees, she frowned at the carpet and began to crawl across the floor. The hem of her dark blue skirt rode up high on her thighs, exposing the dark nylon bands near the top of her panty hose.

Both Wilfred's and Duffy's eyes nearly popped from the sockets as they froze on her shapely legs.

Roy Wilson stepped in quickly behind them, grabbed the file off the desk and stuffed it under his jean jacket.

Paula stuck her head under the desk, then rose to her feet. "Not here," she said, shaking her head.

Red-faced, Duffy still found enough breath to snort piggishly. "Makes you wonder what she was doing under the desk this morning, eh, Ron?'' he said, elbowing his partner lightly in the ribs.

Jack Kiethley was on him like a flash, grabbing the back of his hair with one hand and an ear with the other. He twisted at the waist, and Duffy hit the carpet as if a three-hundred-pound linebacker had just blindsided him. Air rushed from the big OSBI agent's lungs as Kiethley dropped to one knee next to him and drew back a fist.

"Jack, damn it!" Wilson roared, coming around the desk.

"Relax, honey," Paula said. She reached down and ran the back of her hand softly across Jack's cheek, then gently helped her husband back to his feet.

The color returned to Duffy's face, and he lumbered back to his feet.

Paula turned to the big man, smiled up into his eyes, then drove her knee into his groin.

Duffy dropped to his knees coughing, as Paula, her husband and Roy Wilson left the room.

5

Iraj Asal rolled back in his chair and stared at the desk in front of him. Except for the telephone on the right-hand side, the desk top was empty. So were the drawers, the three filing cabinets against the wall and the small storage closet behind him.

Asal's gaze moved to the white letters painted across the picture window just below the drawn shades that faced the parking lot of the small Amarillo shopping center. Windfield Exploration, they read. Nothing more, nothing less. But the name had been enough to fool both Fred Moreland and Skeeter Bradburn, convincing both the Oklahoma Corporation commissioner and the oil-field tool pusher that Windfield was a legitimate Texas oil company intent on moving into Oklahoma and buying information that would give them an upper hand on similar enterprises.

"Windfield Exploration," Asal said out loud, and the words brought a smile to his face. He had picked the name of the company by opening the Amarillo phone book and dropping his finger randomly on the name Windfield, Floyd E. With that name he had gotten a phone installed that enabled both Moreland and Bradburn to call in, further establishing the illu-

sion of reality. It had worked well with Moreland, and
as soon as his part had been played, the commissioner had been silenced.

The smile faded slightly on Asal's face. Habib Harun, Istad Itar's finest pistol shot, had killed the man
while he sat in his office. But it had been Harun's poor
luck to have chosen a moment when the corporation
commissioner sat talking to a man who turned out to
be a police officer. Or something of the sort. That part
of the day's fiasco was still unclear.

Asal slumped in the chair and brought his feet up
onto the edge of the desk, staring at the finely tooled
Western boots that covered his feet. As another part
of the facade, he had played the part most South-
westerners expected out of an Arab oilman opening a
new business in the area. Boots, a Western-cut suit
complete with yoke, and what appeared to be a ninety-
nine gallon hat with a feather band. He had felt silly
in such attire, but the fools in Texas and Oklahoma ate
it up. Everyone had thought the Arab playing cowboy was so "cute," and they had been more than
happy to help him every step of the way.

Asal's thoughts turned to Skeeter Bradburn, a
tougher nut to crack than Moreland. Poor, hungry and
able to get only occasional work since the oil-field
crash, Bradburn had nonetheless been suspicious since
the beginning. He was all too willing to sell secrets for
cash, but when Asal had begun questioning him about
quick routes from one well to the next, Bradburn had
his own questions. And the tone of distrust Asal had
heard over the phone earlier that day convinced the
Istad Itar leader that just as soon as the routes were

worked out, it would be time to send Bradburn's eternal soul to join Fred Moreland's.

Through the window, Asal saw a van pull up and park. Three men got out and started for the front door. The man leading the way was thin, wiry and pale, and a small pencil mustache covered his upper lip. Pierre LaFayette. He had joined the ranks of Istad Itar from the Belgian Communist Fighting Cells.

Just behind LaFayette, Asal saw Skeeter Bradburn. Bradburn's unruly gray hair flopped over his forehead beneath an oil-stained blue-and-white baseball cap. His sky-blue work pants and shirt were equally soiled.

The man at the rear of the procession was tall for an Oriental. Like Asal himself, he wore expensive lizardskin boots. But Rei Yokomoto had chosen faded blue jeans and a matching denim shirt to go with his boots. He represented the Japanese Red Army's contribution to Saddam Hussein's plan to torch the southwestern United States as he had done Kuwait.

LaFayette opened the glass door and ushered Bradburn into the room. Yokomoto followed.

Asal nodded toward the window, and the Japanese jerked the cord on the venetian blinds. LaFayette did the same on the blinds over the glass door.

The room plunged into darkness.

Asal reached behind him and flipped the switch to the overhead light. "Mr. Bradburn," he said, "I will get straight to the point. During our last conversation, I got the feeling that you had more questions you were afraid to ask."

Bradburn had dropped into a metal-and-plastic chair that faced the desk. He sat forward, crossing his arms over his knees defensively. "Why, no, sir," he said in the Texas drawl Asal had learned to hate during his time in the U.S. "I was just wondering why you was needin' to get to the different wells so fast, was all. Seems like you ain't even drilled none, yet." The Texan forced a smile.

"Do we pay you enough, Mr. Bradburn?" Asal asked bluntly.

"Well, sure. I mean, I could always use more. Who couldn't?"

Anger began to boil in the terrorist's blood. He reminded himself that for another day or so, he needed this man. And he reminded himself to stay calm. He *was* calm most of the time, but he had found throughout the years that the wrong combination of events could sometimes suddenly shift him from low gear into overdrive. It didn't happen often, but when it did, the results were always tragic. And bloody.

"Exactly how much more money do you think you are worth?" Asal asked in an even voice.

"Well, sir," Bradburn said. His eyes sparkled suddenly, and Asal could see he thought he had just gained the advantage. "Y'all are givin' me a hundred dollars a day, and that puts biscuits on the table. Ain't too bad for just talkin'. But I been figurin'. You might want to pay me more for something else."

"And what would that be, Mr. Bradburn?"

"*Not* talkin'. To the law. Or maybe to the OSB of I."

Asal pulled his boots off the desk and frowned. "I'm afraid I don't understand."

New confidence filled the tool pusher's eyes. When Bradburn spoke again, his voice was cocky. "Let's toss our cards on the table, Mr. Asal. I've figured out what you're up to. You ain't got no drilling equipment, least not that I've seen. And you ain't got nobody in this outfit that knows a tong jaw from my Aunt Adal's behind." He sat straighter, the irritating accent rising in pitch. "But you want to know how to get to and from wells—other folks' wells—and you want to know how to do it fast." His face beamed with pleasure, now. "It don't take no rocket scientist to figure out what this whole deal's about."

"Oh, really?" Asal said, as it suddenly dawned on him what had happened. Bradburn had been suspicious, all right. But he had no idea what Asal really had planned. The fool thought they were simple oil thieves planning to back trucks up to the tanks in the middle of the night and steal oil.

"Okay," Bradburn said, standing. "Here's what I figure. *I* know the oil patch, and I've even lifted a little crude in my day. I'll help you out, and naturally I don't blow the whistle if I do that. But I ain't gonna do it for no lousy hundred dollars a day."

The accent, combined with the man's newfound arrogance, shot anger through Asal's veins. Common thieves, that's what Bradburn thought they were. Common thieves. The dolt had no idea that they were part of a holy war, that what they were doing had far deeper meaning than stealing oil. Istad Itar was a small finger on the hand of God that would someday destroy the Great Satan America and return the world's power to the Mideast.

As he stared at the man in the chair across from him, a buzzing sound started in Asal's ears. His vision clouded momentarily, and when it returned it had a red tint to it. He felt light-headed, and suddenly it seemed he had divided into two separated entities. One Iraj Asal still stood behind the desk facing Skeeter Bradburn. But another, this one more "intellectual" than physical, stood off to the side, directing the movements of his twin.

"Kill him," Asal heard the intellect whisper.

The body in the chair behind the desk suddenly found itself climbing the barrier between it and Skeeter Bradburn. One of its arms reached under the jacket of his suit and drew the zigzagged blade of a Malaysian dagger from a shoulder sheath.

"Do it," said the part of Asal still standing off to the side and critiquing the performance.

Asal knew his arm was moving, but he felt nothing. Up and down. Up and down. Up and down. Up and down. Over and over the dagger plunged into Bradburn's chest, stomach and arms.

Then, suddenly, he felt two sets of hands clutching him by the arms and pulling him back across the desk.

"Easy, easy," LaFayette said calmly. "He is dead."

Yokomoto guided Asal into the chair where Bradburn had sat. The Istad Itar leader looked down and saw that his suit, shirt, even his slacks were soaked with blood. At his feet he saw what remained of Skeeter Bradburn.

"Go to the hardware store down the street and get a mop and bucket, Rei," LaFayette said, pulling a roll of bills from his pocket and pressing them into the Japanese's hand.

He turned to Asal. "What do you intend to do about the routes now?"

Asal fought the embarrassment he felt over losing control so completely in front of the two men. "We no longer needed him," he said weakly. "We have county maps."

LaFayette shook his head as Yokomoto opened the door, stepped outside, then relocked it behind him. "There could be problems with the maps."

The Arab didn't answer. A sudden peacefulness had come over him, as it always did after an "incident." He felt it sweep through his body, cleansing him, making him feel at peace with the world.

"I said we could have problems," LaFayette repeated. "Things that aren't shown on a map. Perhaps we should find another oil-field worker who knows—"

He was cut off by the shrill ring of the telephone.

BOLAN'S INSTINCTS told him something was wrong as soon as he knocked on the door of room 213 at the Waterford Hotel. When no one answered the door, his suspicions were confirmed.

He glanced up and down the hall. Empty. Turning back to the door, he fished a set of picks from his coat pocket. A second later, the lock clicked. The warrior pocketed the picks and drew the sound-suppressed 9 mm Beretta as he went through the door.

The situation was not as bad as he'd feared.

Roady Rose lay on one of the beds, his eyes closed, the side of his face covered in dried blood. Willem Gerhardt lay on the other bed, his wrists handcuffed to the headboard. He smiled, then shrugged. "A small misunderstanding," he said.

The Executioner holstered the Beretta, then moved to Rose's side. Without speaking, he lifted the man's wrist and checked the pulse. Strong. Steady. He was asleep, not dead or in a coma. Gently Bolan shook the Justice agent's shoulder.

Rose came awake fighting.

The Executioner grasped both of the man's wrists, forcing him back down onto the bed. "Easy. It's me."

Rose's eyes came into focus and he stopped struggling. "Son of a bitch ambushed me."

Bolan nodded. Seeing a half-full glass of water on the nightstand, he handed it to Rose, helped the man into a sitting position, then turned toward Gerhardt.

The Executioner found a handcuff key on the ring to the Blazer and leaned over the German, unlocking the cuffs. Gerhardt sat up, rubbing his wrists.

Bolan grabbed the man under the armpits and jerked him to his feet. "I'm not sure exactly what you tried to pull," the Executioner growled. "But you try anything like it again, you're a dead man."

Gerhardt smirked. "I doubt it. You need me too much."

The Executioner drew the Desert Eagle and jammed the barrel against the German's temple. "I don't need you *that* bad," he said. With his free hand he pulled the Windfield file from under his jacket and dropped it on the bed next to the German. "You ever heard of Windfield Exploration?"

Gerhardt shook his head.

"How about a guy named Iraj Asal?"

"Perhaps."

The Executioner cocked the hammer.

"Yes. I know him. But I do not know where to contact him."

"I do," the Executioner said. Hauling Gerhardt to his feet, he dropped the man on the chair in front of the telephone, then returned to the file on the bed.

The manila folder had contained a list of the most productive wells in Oklahoma. Bolan opened the file and pulled out a scrap of paper. Iraj Asal, it read in what he assumed to be Fred Moreland's handwriting. After that, it said, Windfield Exploration, Amarillo, Texas, and had a phone number preceded by the area code 806. "Call him," he told Gerhardt.

"But... what do I say?"

"Tell him you're here in Oklahoma. You came to help."

Gerhardt shook his head. "It will never work. They will not tell me anything unless they need me for something."

Bolan shoved the Desert Eagle into the man's ribs. "Then you better hope like hell that they need something," he said as he pulled a small cassette recorder and phone jack from his coat.

The Executioner would have preferred to listen on an extension during the call. The problem was, there was no extension. Recording the conversation, and listening later, was the next best thing. "Two rules on this call,'' he told Gerhardt as he hooked the jack to the receiver. "Speak in English. It's a common language between the two of you, and it won't sound suspicious. And rule number two, remember what's going to happen to you if you try anything.''

Gerhardt nodded, his face emotionless.

Bolan switched on the recorder, then dialed the number. A moment later he heard a male voice with a French accent say, "Windfield Exploration. May I help you?'' He handed the phone to Gerhardt, but pressed his ear as close to the receiver as possible.

"Mr. Asal,'' Gerhardt said. There was a pause. "Tell him it is Mr. Wolf.'' He pushed the receiver against his chest and turned to Bolan. "It is a code name. Asal will recognize it.''

Pressing the instrument back to his ear, he said, "Hello, Iraj.''

Bolan could hear only half of the conversation: "Yes... I am well... No, released for lack of evidence.'' Gerhardt laughed. "Yes, Mohammed mentioned it and gave me this number. I am interested.'' A long pause followed during which the Executioner could hear the voice on the other end speaking in a Middle Eastern accent, but couldn't make out the words. Then Gerhardt glanced up at him and answered. "I believe I know a man who could provide such services. A mercenary friend of mine who has worked the oil fields. Would you like me to contact him?'' After another brief interval, the German said, "I will call you back,'' and hung up.

Gerhardt turned to Bolan. "They are progressing with plans for the oil wells. But they have—as you Americans say—run into a slight snag."

The warrior remained silent.

"They had an American oil-field worker on their payroll who was providing them with inside information. Like the corporation commissioner you talked to, he believed he was simply selling information to a competing company intent on stealing."

"What happened?" Rose asked from the other side of the room.

Gerhardt shrugged. "Somehow, he discovered the truth."

"Go on," Bolan prompted.

"Asal killed him, of course."

"And they need to replace him?" Rose queried.

The German nodded.

Bolan turned and faced the wall. Something was starting to smell like a truckload of dead fish, but he couldn't quite put his finger on what. For one thing, if Gerhardt had found an opportunity to jump Rose and beat his head halfway off, he would have had an equal opportunity to kill the Justice agent and escape. So why hadn't he? And this thing about Istad Itar suddenly needing someone who knew the oil fields. The timing seemed a little too convenient.

The Executioner turned back to Gerhardt, studying the man. He was up to something, but there was no way to find out what without playing it out.

Bolan lifted the phone and shoved it into the German's hand. "Call Asal back and tell him you contacted me. Tell him I'm willing to make some extra cash, and tell him one more thing."

"Yes?" Gerhardt asked, taking the receiver from the Executioner.

"Tell him that unlike the guy they killed, I know who I'm dealing with and what's going down. Tell him I don't care as long as the money's right."

6

A fifty-foot statue of a man in boots, jeans and a cowboy hat greeted Bolan and Willem Gerhardt as the Executioner pulled off Interstate 40 into the parking lot of the Big Texan Steak House in Amarillo. Bolan killed the Blazer, pocketed the keys and stepped out of the vehicle. Across the highway, behind a tall chain-link fence, he saw a dark blue Dodge pickup pull into a Texaco station.

Behind the wheel sat Bob "Roady" Rose. The straw cowboy hat on his head looked as if a Brahma bull might have used it for tap-dancing practice, and for all Bolan knew, and considering Rose's bull-riding background, that could have been exactly what had happened.

The warrior led the way to the front door of the steak house, making one final adjustment to the transmitter hidden beneath his denim shirt. He was about to meet Iraj Asal, with Willem Gerhardt providing the introduction and the story that they'd worked together in the past. Rance Pollock would offer to take over where the dead tool pusher had left off, furnishing information about the oil-field sites Istad Itar planned to destroy. In order to tell him what they needed, then determine whether he could be of use to the terrorists, Bolan knew Asal would have to reveal much of the plan.

He already knew what. Now he was looking for when, where, and how.

After the initial interview, Asal would either hire him, or try to kill him to insure his silence. Regardless of what the decision was, the Executioner knew it might be some time before he was able to break away and contact Brognola. So, even though it was risky, he had determined that wearing the ''wire'' was the best course of action. Rose would get the information as quickly as the Executioner himself, and be able to relay it to Brognola via the cellular phone in his pickup. The big Fed could then position the task force of Justice agents and U.S. Army Delta Force soldiers that was already assembling in Washington.

Bolan opened the door for Gerhardt and stepped into the lobby. They walked to a waiter's station, stopped and looked into the main dining room.

A young waitress dressed in a short skirt, plaid Western shirt and a cowboy hat had joined them. ''Two for dinner?'' she inquired, showing an even set of white teeth.

''We are meeting some friends,'' Gerhardt replied.

The waitress beamed again. ''Y'all wanna go in and look?''

''Yes, thank you.'' Gerhardt pushed past the young lady and into the dining room. Bolan followed.

The decor of the Big Texan looked like something from the set of an old John Wayne movie. Wagon wheels hung from the ceiling, light bulbs poking from their spokes. The walls were covered with paintings portraying cattle roundups, gunfights and setting suns, and the rough-hewn tables bore the marks of knives and axes. The waiters and waitresses all wore cowboy gear. The tables were covered with red-and-white checked tablecloths that matched their shirts.

Against the wall at a long table, wearing a Western-cut business suit sat Iraj Asal and four other men.

Bolan let Gerhardt lead the way.

"Iraj," the German said warmly, grasping the Iraqi's hand.

Asal nodded. "Willem."

The warrior studied the man. About five-eight, he could have weighed no more than a hundred and forty pounds. A receding hairline made his forehead look enormous. His smile was pleasant, showing none of the violence or misery the Executioner knew he was capable of inflicting.

"Please, Mr. Pollock," Asal said. "Won't you sit down?" He pointed to the chair across from him. "We have already ordered, and are on our way to the salad bar."

Bolan took a seat, glancing around the table as the men got up. Istad Itar was truly an international assemblage of terrorism's "most valuable players." The Executioner recognized two of them: a thin blond man named Pierre Lafayette of Belgium's Communist Fighting Cells and Rei Yokomoto of the Japanese Red Army.

Those two wouldn't have come cheap. It appeared that Saddam had pulled out all the stops to get the best murderers the world had to offer.

Another of the cowgirl waitresses appeared. Bolan and Gerhardt ordered T-bones as the other men returned to the table, then left for the salad bar.

"Asal is being friendly, of course," Gerhardt whispered. "But I believe he is suspicious. *I* would be in his position. He probably thinks having you show up like this is a little too much like a gift from God."

Bolan nodded. His arrival on the scene *was* a little too convenient. But he didn't know for which side.

Two men with guitars came by the table just after the steaks arrived. One sang a poor rendition of "El Paso" as the men ate, tucked a five-dollar tip from Asal into his shirt, and moved on. Conversation was kept to a minimum. Asal said little, but at one point he set down his fork, looked up at the Executioner and whispered, "Willem tells me you know the oil fields."

Bolan nodded. "Grew up in them. My father was a driller."

"Yes," Asal said. "And you were a Special Forces soldier?"

"Vietnam, Cambodia, Laos. Later I worked Angola and Rhodesia on my own. And Gerhardt's put a dollar or two into my pockets for past services rendered, as well."

Asal cut him off. "I do not doubt your qualifications as a fighting man. Willem would not have brought you if they had not been sufficient. And I am certain you know the oil fields of Oklahoma. The question is, can you be trusted?"

Bolan remained deadpan. "Big money buys big trust."

"Perhaps," the Arab said, then went back to his dinner.

The warrior had just finished his steak when he heard a commotion and turned toward the lobby. He saw a tall burly man in a plaid lumberjack shirt push past two waitresses and weave drunkenly into the dining room. Shoving past another cowgirl who tried to stop him, he hesitated at a table in the center of the room long enough to reach down, grab the meat off the plate of a yuppie-looking man and take a bite. When the man protested, the drunk slapped him across the face with what remained of the steak, laughed uproariously, then wiped his greasy hand on the blouse of the yuppie's date. The woman shrieked.

The drunk reeled toward another table as a tall cowboy across the room stood and made his way forward. "Hey, pard," the cowboy said as he neared the man. "You've had a beer or two too many. How about you and me—"

The big drunk turned and kicked the would-be peacemaker in the groin. The cowboy fell to his knees, moaning in pain.

The waitress who had tried to stop the man hurried to a phone on the wall.

Bolan sat quietly, watching it all.

The drunk made his way on across the room to where the Executioner and the other men sat. His eyes swept the table. "Well, hell," he said in a deep Southern accent. "I ain't never seen this many A-rabs together since *Lawrence of Arabia*." He turned to Bolan. "What you doin' eatin' with a herd of camel jocks?"

The warrior remained silent.

"You gonna answer me, boy?"

When Bolan still didn't speak, the man reared back and threw a big fist toward the Executioner's head.

Bolan reached out, caught it and shoved the man backward.

The drunk fell to a sitting position on the floor.

The Executioner glanced at Asal, who was watching closely.

Bolan didn't hesitate. Standing, he drew the Desert Eagle from under his shirt and pumped two rounds into the drunk's body.

Screams and shrieks erupted around the room as blood poured from the lumberjack shirt. The drunk gasped, vomited, then closed his eyes in death.

Asal rose to his feet. "I suggest we leave before the police arrive," he said calmly.

The room fell silent as they hurried out of the restaurant.

The warrior glanced casually across the interstate as he slid behind the wheel of the Blazer. Rose was still there.

Asal and his men piled into a Ford van and pulled up next to the Blazer. "Follow us," Asal said through the open window, then the van raced toward the highway.

Bolan followed the terrorist vehicle out of the parking lot onto the interstate. A half mile from the Big Texan, six Amarillo PD cars, lights and sirens screaming, passed by on the other side of the median.

Two miles later, the van led the Blazer off the highway onto a county blacktop, and from there to a dirt road. The road turned into a gravel drive that passed a dilapidated farmhouse and led to a barn.

Neither Bolan or Gerhardt had spoken during the fifteen-minute drive into the country, but now, as they followed the van into the barn, Gerhardt said, "I must say I am surprised, Pollock. You killed a harmless drunk just to prove to Asal that you could be trusted." His face beamed with a smile of victory. "It appears that your regard for human life is no better than my own."

"There's a *big* difference," Bolan growled. "I recognized two of the men at the table. LaFayette and Yokomoto. And the guy in the lumberjack shirt was no local drunk."

The Executioner took a deep breath as Asal and his men got out of the van and started for the Blazer. "He was a ringer, Gerhardt. You probably already know him, but in case you don't, the man's name was Sean McVeigh. Provisional Irish Republican Army. He's wanted for murder on three different continents." He lowered his voice as the men neared the car. "At least he was until fifteen minutes ago."

THE FARM WAS one of many that had been abandoned during the 1930s in the dust bowls of the Oklahoma and Texas panhandles. Men and women who had stubbornly refused to give in to the Great Depression, eking a meager existence from the land and waiting for the economy to turn upward once more, found the additional hardship of months without rain finally brought their financial downfall. Eventually they loaded pickups, cars and even horse-drawn wagons with what they could carry and set off for the grape fields of California.

By those standards the men of Istad Itar were living a luxurious, if slovenly, life inside the crumbling old farmhouse, Bolan realized as he followed the terrorists up the rickety steps of the porch and through the front door.

Bare mattresses had been thrown on the floor of the living room. Soiled clothing lay in piles in the corners. Rifles, shotguns and pistols were scattered throughout the room along with ammunition boxes and other accessories.

The dinner they had just finished at the Big Texan appeared to be the first real meal the terrorists had had in some time. There was enough paper refuse littering the floor, bearing the names of several fast-food restaurants, to represent a week's worth of hamburgers and fish and chips.

Bolan followed Asal through the room into the kitchen. The terrorist pulled a lighter from his pocket and lighted the wick of a kerosene lamp on the table. An eerie glow flooded the moldy room as the Executioner took a seat across the table.

Asal stared at him through the semidarkness. "Tell us what you can provide," he said.

"Tell me what you need."

"Information," Asal stated, "concerning the areas around the wells we have chosen." He leaned down to the side of the table, opened a canvas briefcase and pulled out a folded sheet of paper, spreading it out across the table.

Bolan looked down to see a county grid map showing the quarter sections that made up Cimarron—Oklahoma's final county before the Texas, Kansas and Colorado lines appeared. Several *X*s had been drawn on the paper, which he assumed represented wells. They were connected with pencil lines that ran along the county roads.

"When the assault begins," Asal said, "we must be able to move quickly from one well to the next. We must know the fastest routes, and be able to circumvent any unexpected stumbling blocks."

"How many wells is this team responsible for, and how long do you have to torch them?" Bolan asked.

Even in the dim light, the Executioner saw the terrorist's face smile in pride. "There are twenty teams scattered throughout the state. Each team is responsible for twenty-five wells. Each has a team leader, but I am loosely in charge of all—" The smile suddenly fell off his face and his expression turned to one of suspicion. "I will tell you more if we decide to hire you." He twirled the map to face Bolan. "Are you familiar with this area?"

The warrior nodded. "I've been on most of the wells in the entire state at one time or another. Cimarron County I worked two months ago."

Asal's smile returned. "Excellent! Then look at the route I have chosen. See if there is anything I have not taken into consideration."

The Executioner leaned closer to the map, studying the faint pencil lines. Asal had, of course, chosen the most direct routes from well to well.

Arbitrarily picking a well just north of the Cimarron River in the north part of the county, Bolan tapped the map. "Let me see your pencil."

Asal pulled a mechanical pencil from his shirt pocket and handed it across the table.

Bolan erased the existing line that led from the well across a bridge to another *X* just south of the river. He could hear Asal's breathing across the table as he drew a new line that went ten miles west, crossed another bridge, then doubled back along the water to the north well.

"But that is twenty miles out of the way!" Asal said, spinning the map back toward him. "It makes no sense. Why—"

The warrior pointed along the original route. "The flood last April washed that bridge out. The county hasn't rebuilt it yet."

Slowly Asal began to smile. "Yes!" he said excitedly. "Yes! That is exactly the type of information we need!" He calmed slightly, then said, "What of the other routes? Are they—"

The Executioner chuckled good-naturedly. "You haven't given me time to look at them yet."

"Of course." Asal nodded. "Do it now."

Bolan leaned back against the splintered wooden chair, causing it to creak. "Let's talk money first."

The Arab's face hardened. "I will pay you ten thousand dollars to go over the maps and correct mistakes such as this one. Another ten thousand if you will accompany us on the strike in case there are any other unforeseen problems."

Bolan shook his head in the darkness. "Sorry, Asal. I know who's financing you, and he can afford more."

"How much do you want, then?" Asal leaned forward and crossed his arms on the table.

"A hundred grand."

"What! That is impos—"

Bolan cut him off. "Wait a minute. Let me tell you what you'll get for that. First, I'll go over the maps. Tomorrow night, when most of the work around the wells has stopped for the day, I'll drive the route myself to make sure nothing new has occurred since I was on the sites. I'll lead the way when the mission starts, carry my oil-field ID with me in case of problems, and fight alongside you if worse comes to worst."

Asal shook his head. "There is no time to drive the routes before the mission starts. We go tomorrow night."

The warrior hoped Rose had picked that up over the transmitter. Brognola needed that info pronto. But the Executioner knew Rose would have had a hard time following them on the dirt roads without getting spotted, and could easily have lost them somewhere out of transmission range.

Bolan shrugged. "The price is still the same."

Asal leaned closer to the lamp. The Executioner could see the almost caninelike snarl that crept over his face. "Let me make you another offer. We will pay you twenty thousand dollars for the entire job. And you will be allowed to live and spend it."

He surprised the man by laughing. "Hey, you can't blame a guy for trying. Make it thirty thousand and you've got a deal."

Asal smiled slowly. "It is a deal."

Bolan stood. "Then I'll be back tomorrow. What time—"

The Arab reached inside his shirt and came out holding a Walther PPK. LaFayette and Yokomoto suddenly appeared in the kitchen, guns drawn.

"Please sit down," Asal said, aiming his weapon at the Executioner. "You have the maps to reroute." He stepped in, reached under Bolan's shirt and pulled out the Desert Eagle. "Surely you did not believe I could let you go until after the strike had been completed."

7

Roady Rose knew himself pretty well. With one exception, he knew he had never really been afraid of anything in his life.

The exception was failure.

Like the sons of many successful men, Rose had grown up with the gnawing fear that he might never live up to what was expected of the offspring of a well-respected cattle-and-oil man. As a child, that fear had driven him into a make-believe world of Saturday-afternoon Westerns in which he rode the range with Roy Rogers, Dale Evans, Pat Brady and Gabby Hayes. But as he grew older, he had been forced to face reality, and that reality had brought on another type of escape. As soon as he'd finished college, he had been expected to go to work for his father. Instead Roady Rose had entered into a period of womanizing and near alcoholism on the rodeo circuit.

But as he had done so many times when Rose was young, Roy Rogers had saved the day. During a drunken stupor, Rose had written a letter to his childhood hero explaining his fear. Sobering up the next day, he tried desperately to forget he had actually mailed it.

He was shocked when he received a handwritten reply from Rogers a week later. The famous movie cowboy gently recommended that Rose lay off the whiskey, decide what he really wanted to do with his life, then go his own way.

Rose took the man's advice. The thought of a career in law enforcement had played around in the back of his mind, and before he knew it he had sent out an application, been interviewed, then accepted into the Justice Department. The appointment had sent the fear of failure fleeing from the young cowboy's mind.

But now, as Rose peered through the fuzzy image of the night-vision goggles, at the same time doing his best to keep the wheels of the pickup within the deeply grooved ruts of the dirt road, the phantom of inadequacy returned full force.

Rose glanced down at the tape recorder next to the radio receiver as he navigated past the gate to a large cattle ranch. The image was weird, misshapen in the glow of the goggles. But the night-vision instrument didn't affect his hearing, and he knew that the radio receiver was as silent as it had been for the past ten minutes.

The Justice agent sighed as he slowly drove on. He had faced a decision a mile back when he'd seen the van turn off the blacktop onto the county section road. Should he race forward to make sure he stayed within range of Pollock's transmitter? If he did, he risked being spotted by the van. Or should he drop back, insuring his invisibility, but leaving Pollock on his own?

Rose had been a Justice Department agent for more than ten years. He knew that no case was worth the life of a good man, and every fiber in his body screamed that he should cover his partner at all costs. Every fiber but one.

That was the fiber that told him that Rance Pollock wouldn't want him to take the chance of getting spotted. Pollock would be more than willing to give up his own life to save those that would be lost if the oil fields of Oklahoma went up in flames.

So Rose had made his decision accordingly. And now he had to live with it.

He pushed on. Even with the night-vision equipment, his speed was limited to twenty miles an hour, a maddeningly slow pace under the circumstances. The goggles didn't work like they always did on TV and in the movies—or maybe he just hadn't had enough experience with them. In any case, if he sped up he took a chance of sliding down one of the deep embankments that glowed in eerie distortion on both sides of the road. And if that happened, he wouldn't be any good to Pollock or anyone else.

The Justice man saw another ranch entrance ahead. In the fuzzy glow, he could just make out the words on the sign above the cattle guard. The Flying Q. He drove slowly past, winding on up the curving path.

Without warning, he heard a voice over the receiver. The voice disappeared and was replaced by an infuriating static. Rose felt his fists clench around the steering wheel. He was getting close.

Fighting the urge to speed up, the Justice agent lightened his foot on the accelerator. A hundred yards later, he heard the static again, and fifty yards past that he saw another entrance on the opposite side of the road.

Rose sped up slightly. The static increased, then more voices—almost imperceptible in their faintness—worked their way through the noise.

The Justice man turned under a broken and faded sign. Weeds and stray stalks of wild wheat grew up through the rusted cattle guard. The voices rose. He was still unable to make out the words, but one of them sounded like Pollock. His pulse quickening, he continued on.

Rose didn't kid himself. He had another decision to make, one that might well mean the life of the man he had grown to respect so much during the past twenty-four hours. He had to decide exactly how close he should get before he found a place to hide the pickup and listen.

Creeping on in the darkness, the voices cleared further. Here and there, he was able to make out a word or part of a phrase:

" . . . quickly from one well to . . ."

"Twenty teams . . . responsible for twenty-five . . ."

"Look at the routes I have chosen. See if there is anything . . ." The voices faded again into static.

Sweat streamed down his face from under the goggles. It had to be Asal speaking. Twenty teams? Twenty-five wells?

If he'd heard that right, that meant five hundred oil wells in Oklahoma were scheduled to go up in flames.

" . . . I'll even drive the route ahead of time, and I'll lead the way . . ." Pollock's voice.

"There is no time to drive the routes before the mission starts," Asal said. "We go—"

The static returned, as if sent by the devil himself.

Rose slammed a fist onto the steering wheel. The bastard had just told Pollock when the deal was set to go down, and the static had drowned it out. The agent took a deep breath. Well, whenever the time was, it had to be close. And he was close now himself, Rose realized, to wherever Pollock and the men of Istad Itar were holed up. Unless he missed his guess, that would be in one of the abandoned houses or barns so prevalent in the area. Doubt filled him once more. How close was he? Could the terrorists already see him from wherever they were?

The voices from the transmitter cleared suddenly and the static disappeared. Rose pulled immediately to the side of the road. Ripping the night vision goggles from his face, he stuffed them under the seat.

"...surely you did not believe I could let you go until after the strike had been completed?" Rose heard Asal say.

Pollock said simply, and without a trace of fear, "I'd do the same in your shoes."

Rose listened, but it became obvious that the meeting was over. He heard only background voices, mostly in Arabic. He slammed his hand on the steering wheel once more, then opened the glove compartment and pulled out the cellular phone.

A moment later, he heard a sleepy Hal Brognola say, "Hello?"

"It's Rose, sir."

"Where are you?" Brognola sounded suddenly wide-awake.

"South of Amarillo. Pollock's inside an abandoned house with the Istad Itar men."

"Is he all right?"

"I think so," Rose said. "They think he's going to provide info. But they aren't letting him go until after the strike."

"You've been listening in?"

"Yes, sir."

There was a pause. Then Brognola said, "Well, we haven't got all night, Roady. You learned anything new?"

"Sir, if I've picked up things right, Istad Itar has twenty teams ready to move out. They're each responsible for torching twenty-five wells."

Brognola's voice was calm, but Rose could read the tension in it. "They'll be roasting marshmallows across the whole state if that happens. When's it go down?"

Rose felt the lump form in his throat as the feeling that he'd failed returned. "I...I don't know, sir. I lost contact for a while."

A long silence followed. Rose was surprised when the butt-kicking he'd expected didn't come.

"Keep listening," Brognola ordered, "and get back to me just as soon as you have anything else." The Justice man hung up.

Rose had no sooner replaced the phone when he saw the headlights on the road ahead. They flashed across the windshield, illuminating the inside of the pickup.

With no time to hide, the Justice agent switched the receiver off. The tape recorder would pick up anything of importance that he missed, and he could review it just as soon as he'd dealt with whoever was coming down the road.

Dropping his jean jacket over the recorder, he reached under the seat and pulled out a pint bottle of whiskey. A few drops on his T-shirt, and the pickup reeked like the insides of a distillery. Rose took a swig for his breath, spit it onto the seat and drew the SIG-Sauer P-226 from under his waistband and held it out of sight under the open window.

Just a rancher, maybe. It didn't hurt to hope.

The van that had led Pollock and Gerhardt pulled into view, stopped across from him and blew right out the window of the pickup Rose's hopes for a simple encounter with a local.

A dark-complected man got out of the driver's seat and walked toward him. Although he couldn't see in the darkness, Rose heard the door on the other side of the vehicle open.

"You are lost?" the driver asked as he approached the pickup.

Rose forced a drunken slur into his voice. "Damn well certain appears to be a fact." He held up the bottle. "Ol' Jack Daniel done led me astray again." He laughed and extended the bottle out the window, his other hand tightening around the pistol behind the door.

"No, thank you," the man said.

By now a second figure had joined the first. He stood a few feet behind the driver and to the side. His

hand was invisible behind his back. He spoke softly.
In Arabic.

Roady Rose had been making life-and-death decisions all night and he made another one now. At the
very least, these men would go back and tell Asal they
had come across a stranger on the road—a road that
had been deserted for years, and you didn't just
stumble down by accident.

That could spell disaster for Rance Pollock.

Pulling the bottle back inside the pickup, Rose said,
"Oh, well," then pulled the trigger of the P-226. The
first round double-actioned from the barrel through
the pickup door and into the gut of the man outside
the window. Rose jerked the pistol up over the window, gave him two more rounds single-action and
swung the weapon to the second man.

The second man's hand came from behind his back
holding a gun. Rose's next two rounds caught him in
the chest and face before he could fire.

His ears ringing, Rose burst from the pickup and
raced to the van. He ripped open the sliding door to
the rear, then leaped to the side, the P-226 aimed chest
high inside the vehicle.

The van was empty.

Sprinting back to the pickup, the Justice agent
switched the receiver back on. If he was too close to
the house, and Asal and the others had heard the
shots...

The sounds of men snoring was the only noise that
met his ears.

Rose dragged the bodies of the two men to the van,
got behind the wheel and started the engine. He drove

quickly to the nearest ravine, a drop-off of perhaps fifty feet, then slowed. Three seconds before the front wheels went over the side of the road, Rose jumped from the vehicle.

The van plummeted over the embankment and out of sight in the darkness.

Rose sprinted back toward the pickup. Okay, he'd had to cut his losses, and what he'd done wasn't the perfect solution. But there had been no perfect solution under the circumstances. If he and Pollock were lucky, the van wouldn't be found and the men would simply be considered mysteriously missing. If they *were* found, it wouldn't be tonight, and that gave him several hours to find a way out of this mess.

The Justice man slowed, then stopped suddenly when he saw another vehicle parked where the van had stopped. Drawing the SIG-Sauer from his belt, he dived to the side of the road, then crawled forward on his belly.

Slowly the lines of the undercover Justice Department Chevy Blazer appeared across from his pickup.

Rose almost cried out in relief. It was Pollock. Evidently Asal had changed his mind and let him go. The big man had seen the pickup and stopped to find out what was going on.

The Justice agent leaped to his feet, stuck the P-226 back in his belt and jogged toward the Blazer. It wasn't over yet. They still had work to do. If they didn't get both vehicles out of there fast, more terrorists could come along and discover them.

But Rose knew he had done well. He had succeeded. No one could call him a failure.

He reached out, grabbed the door handle and swung the door open.

He was grinning when the hand holding the pistol fired into his chest. The force of the round drove the Justice man back across the road. He backpedaled into the side of the pickup, then raised the P-226 and returned fire.

The body that had been getting out of the driver's side jumped back into the Blazer.

Rose turned and grasped the side of the pickup bed. His eyes were clouding, and for a moment he believed he had the night-vision goggles on again. He looked down at his chest and saw blood gushing from the hole in the center. His arms felt as if someone had bored holes through the bones and poured molten lead into the cavities.

Slowly Rose pulled himself along the pickup bed toward the cab. He knew he was dying, but he knew there was one thing he had to do before he gave in to death.

Another shot exploded from the Blazer as Rose opened the door to the pickup. The round caught him in the back of the calf. A high-pitched scream escaped his lips. Another round drilled into his back as he leaned over the seat and pulled his jacket away from the recorder.

The men were out of the Blazer now. Rose could hear their feet on the hard-packed dirt. He forced his gun hand up again, and let the barrel rest on the tape recorder.

A volley of automatic fire ripped through him a second before he pulled the trigger of the P-226.

Rose saw the tape recorder burst into pieces. Then his eyes closed, and he slid to the dirt on the Texas Panhandle road.

HAL BROGNOLA SAT on the edge of the bed, staring through the dim glow of the lamp on the nightstand. There, next to the lamp, waiting in frustrating silence, he saw the cordless phone in the charger.

The big Fed glanced over his shoulder and smiled. His wife had awakened momentarily when the telephone rang. But a career of late-night "wake-up" calls had taught her to awaken, ascertain whether her husband would be leaving, then fall back asleep immediately.

Rising quietly to his feet, the Justice man lifted the phone from the charger and padded barefoot across the bedroom, down the hall and into his den. He twisted the switch on the floor lamp by his reclining chair and sat down.

Brognola glanced at the clock on the wall. It had been half an hour since the phone had awakened him. Rose should be calling back with more information soon. He closed his eyes.

The big Fed awoke with a start and jerked his gaze back to the clock. He was surprised to see now that it had been more than an hour since he'd talked to Rose. Should he call the agent on the cellular phone? No, not yet. There could be any number of reasons that the man hadn't called in yet. He could be in the middle of learning new information and waiting for a dull spot before phoning. Or he might even be in a position where he had to maintain silence in order not to be detected. If that was the case, a call from Brognola could jeopardize his position.

Brognola frowned. He had called the Oklahoma Bureau of Investigation a few hours earlier, been informed that the man was out of town and talked to the deputy director—J. D. Baker. Brognola had advised Baker of the situation and informed him that a combined task force of Justice Department agents and Delta Force soldiers was in transit to Oklahoma City. Baker had promised to provide OSBI agents who knew the area. By now, they would all be gathering at OSBI headquarters and arming up for the joint mission.

The phone rang shrilly, causing Brognola to jump in his chair. Snatching it up off the table next to him, he thumbed the on-off button and said, "Hello?"

A few seconds of silence followed. Then a frightened adolescent-sounding voice said, "I know it's late and I'm sorry to wake you up, Mr. Zeiler, but Erica and I had sort of a fight this evening. Is there any way I could talk to her? I know—"

"You've got the wrong damn number!" Brognola shouted into the mouthpiece and thumbed the button again.

Impatient now, he stared back to the clock. Almost an hour and a half. Too long. It was time to risk a call.

Tapping in the number of Rose's cellular phone, the Justice man heard the line connect. A moment later, he heard it ring.

And ring.

Brognola was about to hang up when the line clicked open. "Hello?" he said. "Hello?"

There was no answer.

The big Fed waited, a sick feeling creeping down his abdomen as the silence seemed to get louder. He pressed the phone tighter to his ear. He couldn't be sure, but it sounded like someone was whispering in the background.

Then a voice came on the line. "Hello?"

Brognola knew the voice. Most of the time, he welcomed hearing it. But right now, with what he knew from Rose, hearing it not only made no sense, it was the last voice he had expected, or wanted, to hear.

"Hello," Mack Bolan said again into the cellular phone.

ON HIS BACK on the bare mattress in the middle of the living-room floor, the Executioner looked up at the cracks in the farmhouse ceiling. Next to him, on a similar mattress, he could hear Willem Gerhardt snoring the sleep of the dead, as well as the slumber sounds of other terrorists.

Several terrorists stood guard around the farmhouse and barn. Bolan had seen the van leave earlier, while he was still poring over the maps of Oklahoma's counties. Then Asal had demanded he give up the keys to the Blazer, and a few minutes after that the Executioner's own vehicle had driven off.

The warrior glanced around the room. The old farmhouse had been built before indoor plumbing had become common in the Southwest. The concrete foundation for an outhouse still stood twenty yards to the rear of the structure, but the tiny building that had once sprouted above the twin holes in the concrete had long ago rotted away.

Whether the terrorists were too modest to perform their bodily functions in the great outdoors, or simply too lazy to walk the twenty yards to the concrete toilets, Bolan didn't know. In any case, a hole in the floor of a rear bedroom had been turned into a rest room by the terrorists, and it was in that direction that Bolan had been led when he'd told Asal that the call of nature was upon him.

Not that the Executioner had needed to be told the way. He could well have followed his nose. The stench had been overpowering when he'd entered the room, but the Executioner had been thankful for it. The guard Asal had assigned to watch him had stopped in the hall, which gave Bolan ample opportunity to toss the hidden transmitter into the pile of human feces and let it roll out of sight beneath the house.

The warrior had hated losing his only communication with the outside world, but Asal was already suspicious. Otherwise he wouldn't have insisted on Bolan remaining at the house. And if anything else happened to increase those suspicions, it seemed likely that a "bug check" might be initiated.

As he lay staring at the ceiling, remembering the transmitter, Bolan's thoughts turned back to Roady Rose. The transmitter would pick up nothing from its current location. But everything had already been said that could benefit Brognola, and Rose had either gotten it or hadn't. The Executioner hadn't seen the pickup's headlights since they'd turned off the county blacktop onto the dirt road, and knew it was likely that the Justice agent had lost them. Even if Rose had been out of range for only a short period of time, the radio silence might well have come during the crucial period of his conversation with Asal.

If it had, Brognola still didn't know when the torch jobs were scheduled to go down.

There was no way to know, and only one answer to the dilemma. Hope for the best, but prepare for the worst. Proceed with the mission, assuming that Brognola still didn't know how soon the strike would go down, and find some other way to contact the Justice man at the earliest opportunity.

Asal entered the living room, breaking into the Executioner's thoughts. "You are rested?"

Bolan nodded. He noted that the terrorist still carried the Desert Eagle in his waistband.

"Then you must finish the routes." The leader of Istad Itar stepped back as the Executioner got to his feet.

Bolan stepped over Gerhardt and followed Asal toward the kitchen. He was halfway there when headlights appeared in the front yard.

The Blazer parked next to the front porch.

The warrior frowned. Where was the van?

"Come," Asal said, taking his arm and pulling him toward the kitchen. "You have work to do."

Bolan sat at the kitchen table, opened another of the county grid maps and lifted the pencil. He had gone over two dozen of the maps earlier, drawing long circuitous courses between as many of the wells as he thought he could get by with. He had invented stories similar to the one about the washed-out bridge for each detour. There were no guarantees on this mission, and the task force might not get word of the exact site locations until the strike was already underway. If that happened, anything that slowed the progress of the terrorists would be an advantage.

The Executioner had started to draw a line between two wells in Woods County, when the front door opened and a man hurried in and whispered into Asal's ear. The Iraqi barked something in Arabic, then turned to the Executioner.

A moment later, three more men entered the kitchen carrying a fourth. They dropped the body on the floor.

Bolan glanced down. Half of the man's head had been blown away, and the rest of his body had been saturated with gunfire. But the Executioner could see the remnants of the black T-shirt, cowboy boots and faded Levi's jeans.

Hard waves of fury swept through him as he stared at what remained of Roady Rose. He fought the temptation to rise from his chair, snatch the Desert Eagle from Asal's belt and kill them all.

But he couldn't. Not if he wanted to stop the strike. He might kill these men, but if he did he would never learn the exact location of the other wells scattered across Oklahoma.

Asal stepped forward, staring at Bolan. "Who is this man?" he demanded.

Bolan shrugged. "How am I supposed to know?" he forced himself to say. He turned back to the map in front of him.

Behind Asal, the men who had carried the body now drew weapons and aimed them at the Executioner.

"Do not lie to me!" Asal shouted. "Who are you? FBI?"

The warrior looked back up. "Are you nuts?" he asked calmly.

Asal turned to the men behind him as one of them pulled the radio receiver from his pocket. Another held out the mangled remnants of a tape recorder. Still a third held the cellular phone from inside Rose's pickup.

"Search him!" Asal ordered. He turned and yelled through the door to the living room. "Bring Gerhardt in here!"

Two of the three men stepped forward and pressed the barrels of their pistols into the Executioner's ear. The third leaned down, ripping the snaps down the front of Bolan's shirt and running his arms across his chest. He turned back to Asal and shook his head.

The Iraqi's eyes clouded in doubt as Gerhardt walked sleepily into the kitchen.

Asal slapped the German across the face. "Who is this man?"

Gerhardt showed no emotion as he rubbed his cheek. "What are you talking about? I told you who he was."

The Arab stuck the receiver in Gerhardt's face. "This man," he said, pointing to the floor, "was outside listening and recording." He reached up and ripped Gerhardt's shirt from his back. Again finding no transmitter, he turned back to Bolan.

"Where is it?"

"I've got to assume you're talking about a bug of some sort," Bolan said, "and I don't know anything about it."

By now, most of the men on the living-room floor had awakened. They stood crowding the door to the kitchen. Asal stomped toward them. "There is a transmitter hidden somewhere in this house!" he shouted. "Find it!"

The men dispersed throughout the house.

"You mind if I get back to work?" Bolan asked.

Asal glared at him. "If we find that you have betrayed us, American," he said. "You and—" he turned to Gerhardt "—*you* will die a slow and painful death."

Bolan nodded. "Sounds fair enough to me. But that's not what you're going to find." He returned to the map.

The Executioner listened to the sounds of the men ransacking the house as he continued to draw routes on the map. He didn't think it likely that they'd find the transmitter. Not only would no one want to sift through the reeking pile of feces under the house, they were under the impression that Bolan, or at least *someone*, had planted the bug. They would know it wouldn't function from under the house, and therefore not bother to look for it there.

Bolan drew on, coming up with imaginary deterrents to logical routes between wells, and waiting. The men in the kitchen moved back across the room but kept their weapons aimed at him.

An hour later, Asal came back to the kitchen.

Bolan looked up. "Find anything?"

The Arab didn't answer. He looked quickly to what remained of the tape recorder and had started to speak when the cellular phone suddenly rang.

"Do I answer it?" the terrorist holding it asked uncertainly.

Asal hesitated. "No. They will recognize the accent."

He pointed to Bolan. "You."

The warrior shook his head. "I don't know who it is."

Asal stepped in and slapped him across the face. He drew a dagger from under his shirt and held it to the Executioner's throat. "Maybe you know who it is, and maybe you do not. But you will answer it anyway. Make up something about finding the phone. Tell them something, and find out who they are."

The man holding the cellular licked the suction cup on a phone jack and pressed it onto the instrument. He plugged the other end into a tape recorder.

"Make it convincing," Asal said, "or you will find yourself on the floor next to this man."

8

Bolan took the cellular phone and tapped the button, answering the call. "Hello?" he said. There was a long pause, and for a moment he wondered if Brognola had hung up. "Hello?" he repeated.

The familiar voice of the Justice man finally answered. "Hello."

Bolan glanced at Asal. Brognola already had the list of high-producing wells, and therefore had a general idea of where the terrorists would strike. But the operative word was general, and the Executioner's old friend would need more specific intel to be a hundred-percent effective. Asal and his men weren't only listening, however, they were recording the conversation so they could hear the other end later. They'd not only hear what Brognola had to say, they'd have a chance to play it over and over, studying it for double meanings.

The Executioner knew the specifics would have to wait. He'd be lucky right now to convey what had happened to Rose and get Brognola to convince Asal that the surveillance had been directed somewhere else.

As if to emphasize his thoughts, one of the terrorists moved in closer and jammed a revolver into his ribs. If the ruse didn't work, Bolan knew he'd never stand up from the table.

"Who am I speaking to?" the Executioner said into the phone.

"Who am *I* speaking to?"

Bolan realized immediately that Brognola had picked up on what was going on. There was no way the big Fed man wouldn't have recognized his voice, and Brognola knew the Executioner had to have recognized his. He was throwing the ball back into Bolan's court, waiting to get a few more details before jumping in too deeply.

"This is Detective Sergeant Leonard Tillis," Bolan replied. "Amarillo Police Department."

Asal gasped. The man with the gun in the Executioner's ribs cocked the hammer.

"Stand by a moment," Bolan said into the cellular phone. He covered the mouthpiece with his hand. "Look," he told Asal, glancing at the body on the floor, "we know this guy was a cop of some type, or he wouldn't have had the recorder or bug." He raised the phone slightly. "Which means whoever this is on the phone is a cop, too. Probably his boss. Right?"

Asal's face was a mask of suspicion.

"If you want to find out who they are, and what they know, let me handle it my way. Who do you think a cop is more likely to talk to, another cop or whoever killed his man?"

Slowly Asal nodded. But he kept the razor point of the dagger against Bolan's throat as he said, "Continue. But be *very* careful."

Bolan turned back to the phone. "Sorry for the interruption," he said. "We're running around out here like chickens with our heads cut off. I'm sorry to have to tell you this, but your man's dead."

"Dead?" Brognola repeated.

"Yeah. Found him shot in his pickup just inside the city limits. Looks like he was driven there and dumped after he died, but other than that we haven't a clue to go on. No ID, but we figured from the equipment in his vehicle that he had to be some kind of cop running surveillance on somebody." Bolan paused. Brognola now had everything necessary to figure out the situation and what was needed from him. It was time for the G-man to get into the act.

"But I'm getting ahead of myself," Bolan said. "Who did you say you were?"

Brognola cleared his throat. "Francis Lupo. Special agent in charge of the Dallas office, DEA."

"Like I said, Agent Lupo, we don't have much to go on. Care to shed a little light on the subject for us?"

Brognola cleared his throat again. There was another pause, and Bolan could almost see the gears in his old friend's head working. "Sorry," the G-man finally said. "The news shook me up. The man you found was one of our agents, all right. Tim Bradley. He was a good man."

"I'm sorry," Bolan said. "Can you tell me what he was working on? Something to get us started on the investigation?"

"You bet I can," Brognola said, playing along. "There's a methamphetamine lab just outside Amarillo set up in one of the ranch houses. They're supplying half the state. Bradley was running surveillance on an undercover buy. The undercover man called in earlier and said he never showed up to meet him after the deal went down. Sounds like the dopers caught him somewhere on the road."

"That's a start," Bolan said. "You got a number where I can reach you?"

"Sure thing." Brognola rattled off a number with a 214 area code. Bolan lifted the pencil and wrote it down on the faded wood of the table. He had no doubt it would link them to the real DEA office in Dallas if the terrorists called to check, but before that could happen Brognola would have called there to set up a cover.

"I'll get back to you as soon as we learn something. At least by tomorrow," Bolan said. He tapped the channel button on the phone and heard the beep as the call changed frequencies. "Sorry," he said. "Accidentally hit a button. You still there?"

"Yes."

"You hear what I said? I'll get back to you by tomorrow night," Bolan repeated, hoping the terrorists didn't catch the emphasis he was putting on the time. "Sooner if we come up with something."

"Got you, Sargeant. One other thing."

Bolan waited.

Brognola took a deep breath, and when he spoke the Executioner knew he was no longer acting. "Like I said, Bradley was a damn good man. I want you to get whoever killed him."

The Executioner glanced around the room at the terrorists. "We'll have them in custody by tomorrow night, Agent Lupo," he said. "Count on it." He tapped the button and hung up.

Asal pulled the dagger away from the Executioner's throat and nodded to the man who had hooked up the recorder. The man pulled the suction cup from the instrument, rewound the tape and played back the recording.

"Perhaps you are telling the truth," Asal said skeptically after they'd reviewed the conversation.

Bolan shrugged. "Hey, chalk it up to bad luck. You had no way of knowing there was a drug lab somewhere around here."

Asal nodded. "We will watch you closely anyway, just to make sure." He tapped the map on the kitchen table. "Now get back to work. We are running out of time."

THE MAPS TOOK the better part of the night, but by the time dawn rose over the Texas Panhandle Bolan had completed routes that linked the other wells scattered across Oklahoma's seventy-seven counties. Asal had stood behind him, patiently waiting. He asked an occasional question, then made notes in a small notebook. It was obvious he was waiting until the task was complete, then planning to relay the information to the leaders of the nineteen other teams hiding somewhere around the strike sites.

Bolan rose from the table. "I'd better catch some shut-eye," he said as the Istad Itar leader shuffled the maps into a stack.

"Some what?" Asal asked, puzzled.

"Shut-eye," Bolan repeated. "It's slang for sleep." He started for the door to the living room, then turned back. "When do we leave?"

Asal stood, tucking the maps under his arm. "Noon," he said as he passed the Executioner and proceeded out the front door.

The warrior watched him step up into the van. Several of the men had retrieved it from the ravine during the night, and except for a few scratches in the paint job, the vehicle had been no worse for wear. The Executioner dropped down onto the mattress as Asal pulled away.

He didn't know exactly where the Iraqi was heading, but he'd bet his last bullet that wherever it was, they had a fax machine.

Which was exactly what *he* needed.

The Executioner lay back on the mattress and closed his eyes. Around him, he could hear the breathing of the men still asleep, Gerhardt among them. He dozed lightly, still aware of everything around him, and let his mind drift over what had to be accomplished in the next few hours.

From what he had picked up from comments here and there throughout the night, he knew the massive torch job was set to begin just after dark. That would be in the neighborhood of 2100 hours tonight. Brognola needed to be made aware of that fact. He also needed to know what method the terrorists planned to use to set the fires. And he still needed to know which specific wells were on the agenda.

Vehicle engines hummed outside the window, and Bolan looked through the glass to see ten pickups pulling up in front of the house. The noise woke the sleeping men, and one by one they began to rise and prepare for the day.

Gerhardt woke up, rolled to his side and whispered, "It went well?"

Bolan nodded.

The German glanced quickly around the room to make sure no one was watching. "Then soon it will be over," he said. "And then you will set me free."

Bolan felt anger rise within him. He didn't like the German, and he didn't like cutting deals with terrorists. But the Executioner had been around long enough to know that sometimes it became necessary. You had to go with the lesser of two evils—lose the battle to win the war.

He stared Gerhardt in the eye. "Soon it will be over, yes. But *I* don't set you free. I turn you back over to the man Rose worked for. What he does is up to him."

A look of concern crossed Gerhardt's face. "He would not have lied to me, would he?"

Bolan shook his head. "He never has."

A thin figure crossed the room and stopped at the Executioner's feet. "Get up," LaFayette said in heavily accented English. "Both of you. We are about to load the trucks."

The warrior glanced at the pickups in the front yard. He still didn't know the method Asal and his men planned to use to start the fires, and the equipment they loaded might give him a clue. But it wouldn't do to look too eager.

The Executioner shook his head. "We didn't sign on as laborers."

Lafayette's thin lips rose, taking the pencil mustache with them. He drew a 9 mm Browning Hi-Power pistol from under his jacket, aimed it at the Executioner and cocked the hammer. "Your contract has been changed," he snarled.

Bolan smiled. "The terms seem fair enough." He rose to his feet. "Just show me the way."

Lafayette led the two men out the door. The pickups had formed a line leading to the barn. The men were carrying crates and boxes out of the door to the first truck, which had backed up to the entrance.

The Belgian led them around the truck and into the barn. Three stacks of boxes sat against the wall under the splintering hayloft. Invisible in the darkness the night before, Bolan now saw that the first stack was composed of crates containing AK-47s. The second held crates of ammo.

The third pile was made up of ten pine crates that were marked with the words *Pancerovka*, and P-27. The emblem of the former nation of Czechoslovakia was also imprinted in the wood.

Bolan nodded. Rocket launchers. It made sense. No one in his right mind would want to be too close when the fires started. But if someone stole onto the lease and opened the dual completion valve in the wellhead, he could then retreat to a safe distance and—

"You!" Lafayette growled, pointing at Bolan. "One crate from each pile onto the trucks."

Bolan nodded, walking directly to the pile of P-27s. He lifted one off the top and moved it to the doorway, waiting for the next truck in line to back up. Behind him, he heard Gerhardt and another man struggling with a case of rifles.

Okay, the Executioner thought as he dropped the rocket launcher on the tailgate of the pickup and shoved it forward. He knew what, where, when, and now even how.

Now to get that information to Brognola.

They had finished loading the pickups and were on their way back to the house when Asal returned in the van. The Istad Itar leader was grinning like a cat who'd just cornered a mouse.

Bolan broke off from his path to the house and walked to meet Asal. "We need to talk," he said.

The smile faded from the Iraqi's face.

"I'm supposed to call that DEA guy back tonight," the Executioner said. "If I don't, he'll call the Amarillo PD and find out there is no Detective Sergeant Leonard Tillis, and no report of a body."

Asal shook his head. "It does not matter. By that time, we will be lighting the fires."

"Oh, it matters all right," Bolan said. "I know American cops, Asal. I know how they think. You kill one of them and the rest take it very personally." He stared straight into the terrorist's eyes. "Let me tell you what's going to happen. This Francis Lupo is going to get impatient. He's going to call the PD *this morning*. He's going to want to send some of his own men to help with the investigation—the only reason he didn't do it last night was because I told him we'd have them in custody fast."

Wrinkle lines formed in the corners of Asal's eyes. "They will not know where to look."

"Asal, think about it," Bolan said. "The drug lab that this Bradley guy was watching must be just down the road. They're gonna go over this countryside with a fine-tooth comb. And that includes this place." He paused to let it sink in.

The Arab looked at him skeptically. "What do you suggest?"

"I'll go in and call him back at the number he gave me. Tell him we've got two men in custody, and he should fly out if he wants. That'll keep him busy and keep him from contacting the Amarillo cops directly. By the time he gets off the plane, it *will* be too late."

Asal stared up at the Executioner, thinking. Finally he said, "Do it."

Bolan led him into the house to the kitchen table where Rose's cellular phone still lay. He squinted down at the number on the table for Asal's benefit, then tapped in another set of digits.

Like most police agencies around the U.S., Hal Brognola's phone system contained what was known as a "Hello" line. It was used exclusively for undercover ops, and answered accordingly.

Bolan recognized the voice of Brognola's secretary as she picked up the phone in Washington. "Dallas DEA," she said. "How may I direct your call?"

"Special Agent in Charge Francis Lupo," Bolan said.

"May I tell him who's calling?"

"Detective Sergeant Leonard Tillis," Bolan said, "Amarillo PD."

"Please hold."

A moment later, Brognola came on. "Yes, Sergeant?" he said. "What have you got?"

"Good news." Bolan glanced at Asal and nodded. In the hustle and bustle of the morning, the terrorist leader had forgotten about hooking up the tape recorder. He wouldn't be able to hear Brognola's end, or listen to what the Executioner said more than once. That would give him a little more leeway.

With heavy emphasis on the word *little*.

"We've got several men in custody," Bolan said. "Took down the house on probable cause. The lab's there, all right, and I've got uniformed men securing the place until you boys can get out and process it."

"That's great," Brognola said. "What else can you tell me?"

"We'll be piecing things together the rest of the day. You're welcome to come on out if you like."

Brognola didn't answer right away, and Bolan knew he was trying to decide what the Executioner wanted him to say. There was no way to give him any further clue without alerting Asal, so the warrior waited.

The Justice man made the right decision. "Naturally I want my men in on this," he said. "Tim was one of ours, after all. But we're tied up on a cocaine deal right here this afternoon and tonight, and it sounds like you've got everything under control. I'll fly out personally in the morning."

"You'll be met at the airport," Bolan said. "I'll get back to you by phone as soon as we know anything else."

Brognola coughed over the line. "Remember we've got a bust going down here. But I definitely will find a way to take your call. Any idea when that call might be?" he asked, giving the Executioner the opening he needed.

"Probably late tonight," Bolan said. "I'll be tied up myself during the early part of the evening." He glanced at Asal out of the corner of his eye and saw the man's face harden slightly.

Bolan knew he had pressed his luck to the breaking point. "Now, if you'll excuse me, Agent Lupo," he said, "I've got some murder suspects to interrogate."

"Go to it," Brognola answered. "Tell me, what kind of sentence are they likely to get up there? I don't know any of the judges in the Panhandle."

"I do," Bolan said, "and I'd say there's a fine chance that the Tim Bradley's murderers will be executed."

The look of suspicion still covered Asal's face as the warrior set the phone back down on the table. "There was a lot of things you did not have to say," the terrorist stated.

"It's called bullshit, Asal," Bolan said offhandedly. "Cop bullshit. If I hadn't done it, he'd have thought it was strange." He pointed to the Desert Eagle still in the Iraqi's belt. "Look, I've done everything you wanted, and I've done it well. Now, how about giving me my piece back?"

"I do not think so. Not quite yet."

Bolan shrugged.

An hour later the trucks were loaded and Asal ordered the men into formation in the front yard. The canvas briefcase that had been in the kitchen now hung over his shoulder by a strap, and Bolan could see the stack of county maps extending through the open top. The fact that he still had them meant that Asal had faxed their images to the leaders of the other Istad Itar teams.

"To avoid suspicion on the highway," the terrorist leader began, "only two men will ride in each pickup. The rest of you will follow in the van and the Blazer. We will hide those vehicles at a spot I have chosen near the first well. As soon as darkness falls, the men in them will climb into the back of the pickups and we will begin."

"Do you expect problems?" someone asked.

"It is a precautionary measure only," Asal replied, pacing back and forth in front of the assembled men. "The only problems we might encounter would be some workers left at the wells or perhaps a highway patrolman."

"If that happens—" the same man started to say.

"Kill them," Asal finished for him. Pulling five bundles of paper from a side pocket of the briefcase, he handed one each to LaFayette and Yokomoto, then gave the remainders to three other men. "These are the assignments. There will be two pickups in each team— one responsible for igniting the fire, the other serving as backup in case there is an equipment malfunction. Each team will set fire to five wells. There will be a driver in each truck. The other man will serve as navigator. You have been provided with a map of your area, and the routes Mr. Pollock has provided for us." He paused, then said, "We will not meet again when this is over. Take the route you have decided on to wherever you have decided to go. You are to contact the headquarters in Baghdad for payment in two weeks."

Asal didn't ask if there were any questions. He pivoted on his heel like some third-world despot and headed toward the Blazer.

Voices in a variety of languages murmured in the front yard of the farmhouse as the subteam leaders identified those in their unit and headed toward the pickups. Rei Yokomoto looked across the grass to Bolan. "Pollock," he said, glancing down at the sheaf of papers in his hand, "you are with me in the lead vehicle."

Bolan watched Gerhardt get into the Bronco with Asal as he followed the Japanese Red Army man to a blue Ford that faced the road. He took the passenger's seat.

Yokomoto's jean jacket whipped back slightly in the wind as he opened the driver's door. Bolan saw the leather strap of a shoulder holster under his arm. The Executioner made a mental note, then settled in for the ride.

The Japanese took his seat and turned to Bolan. "Asal does not completely trust you," he said. "Therefore, *I* do not trust you at all." He paused, then started the engine. "The slightest wrong move on your part will result in your death," he finished, then led the caravan out the drive, and down the county road to Highway 287.

The other vehicles dropped back, keeping a quarter mile or so between them to avoid suspicion as they headed north across the Canadian River. Yokomoto leaned across the cab, flipped open the glove compartment and produced a walkie-talkie. Switching it on, he adjusted the squelch and set it on the seat between them.

Little was said as the procession passed through Dumas, Texas, then followed the highway across the state line. It was late afternoon when they saw the outskirts of Boise City, Oklahoma.

From somewhere behind them, Asal's voice came over the radio. "LaFayette. There is a convenience store a few blocks down the intersecting highway. Go there and buy enough food for the men."

The Belgian acknowledged the order.

"The rest of you," Asal went on, "divide up and go to the various gas stations. Be sure your tanks are full."

Bolan's mind raced as they entered the small town and Yokomoto guided the Ford into a Phillips 66 station. By now, the counterterrorist task force teams would be assembled. Brognola would have divided up the state and sent teams to wait in each sector. But the task force still didn't know the exact wells. They could guess, they could gamble, and they could play the odds. And they would guess right on many of the wells, but not all of them.

They'd be close. But not close enough. Some wells would be torched before they could stop the terrorists.

"Stay inside the truck," Yokomoto ordered as he parked next to the self-service pump. He got out.

Bolan glanced down at the map of Cimarron County next to him on the seat. The wells Asal's men were responsible for lay only a few miles north of Boise City. This would be his last chance to get the information to Brognola before they holed up in the woods somewhere and waited for the sun to set.

The Executioner looked out at the sporadic traffic on the highway as Yokomoto filled the tank. Several cars and pickups passed the station. A small white Datsun with the stenciled word Police marking the door pulled in next to a pump.

A man wearing a khaki shirt, blue jeans and a black Sam Browne belt bearing a .357 Magnum revolver got out. He nodded to Yokomoto, then stuck the nozzle of the other pump into his car.

Bolan looked up into the rearview mirror. There was no way he could talk to the cop without Yokomoto seeing him.

The police officer and terrorist finished at the same time, hung their pumps back on the tanks and started into the station. As they went inside, the warrior heard the screech of rubber and looked to his side to see a ten- or eleven-year-old boy skid to a stop on his bicycle.

The kid wore ragged jeans, worn-out running shoes and a striped T-shirt. He dropped to his knees, twisted the cap off his rear tire and stuck the air-hose nozzle against the tube.

Air hissed from the hose to the side of the tire. The kid readjusted the nozzle and tried again with no better luck. "Fuck," the kid said under his breath.

Bolan grinned as he ripped a small scrap of paper off the map next to him. Maybe he should come back later and wash the kid's mouth out with soap, but if the boy could pull off what the Executioner was about to ask of him, he'd acquit him on all profanity charges. Quickly writing Brognola's number down, the warrior pulled a twenty-dollar bill from his pocket, palmed both papers and exited the vehicle.

He could see Yokomoto glaring at him through the window of the station as the Japanese terrorist waited for the cop to pay.

Bolan squatted next to the boy. He knew he had only seconds before Yokomoto would be back. "Need help, son?" he asked.

The boy looked up and nodded.

The Executioner stuck the nozzle onto the tire. As it filled, he let the scrap of paper drop from his hand to the ground. "Listen carefully," he told the boy. "On the paper I just dropped there's a number. I want you to call it for me. All you've got to remember to say is this—Striker says sundown. He'll get maps to you as soon as he can." He paused. "Can you say that?"

"What are you?" the boy asked, looking up in awe. "Some kind of spy?"

Bolan nodded. "Exactly. And I need your help." He dropped the twenty next to the scrap of paper.

The kid looked down and grinned.

"Repeat back to me what I told you," Bolan said.

"Striker says sundown. He'll get maps to you soon."

"Close enough," Bolan told him. He finished the tire and screwed the cap back on as the kid pocketed the money and number. "One other thing. The man with me doesn't know what we're doing. Let's keep it that way."

The kid frowned, and Bolan could almost see his brain working behind his squinted eyes. "That'll cost you extra," he finally said.

The Executioner stifled a smile. The kid had spunk. "How about you do it, and I won't tell your mother what you said when you couldn't get the hose to work?"

The boy's eyes opened wide. "You got a deal."

Yokomoto was exiting the station as Bolan rose and walked back to the pickup. He slid behind the wheel and inserted the key. "You are a true humanitarian," the Japanese said sarcastically.

Bolan shrugged.

Another of the trucks was pulling in as they left the station and started north.

Bolan sat back against the seat. Asal still had the route maps, but there was no way the Executioner would have entrusted them to a ten-year-old even if they'd been in his possession. But the fact remained that in less than three hours the fires would start, and Brognola still didn't know where.

It all boiled down to the fact that Bolan had racked his brain for a plan to get the routes to the big Fed during the entire drive. He had come up with only one possible solution under the circumstances.

The Executioner was about to start executing.

HAL BROGNOLA stared through the fifth-floor window of the OSBI deputy director's office at the rush-hour traffic on the Broadway Extension.

Next to Brognola, J. D. Baker said, "He's here. One moment," then handed the Justice man the phone. "Your Washington office."

"Damn it, Kelly," Brognola said, pressing the phone to his ear, "I told you to hold my calls."

"I'm sorry, Hal, but this one was special. A little boy. Said his name was Randy Boyle."

"What?" Brognola said around the chewed stump of his cigar.

"He said to tell you 'Striker says sundown. And that he'd get maps to you soon.'"

Brognola bit the cigar in half and it fell to the floor of the office. "Where'd the call come in from?"

"Boise City. It's in the northwest corner of the Panhandle near the Colorado, New Mexico and Kansas lines."

"Did the kid say anything else?"

"Just that the man gave him twenty dollars to make the call. He wondered if you might want to give him some more."

Brognola didn't answer. Dropping the phone back in the cradle, he lifted it again and tapped in another number. "Get on the horn, Wilson," he said. "Tell everybody the wells go up at sundown. Tell them we're still waiting on exact site locations, but we might get those soon."

"And what if we don't?" Roy Wilson asked.

Brognola hesitated, then said, "Then I guess we start following the flames."

IT WAS nearly 1800 hours when Yokomoto steered the pickup off the highway onto a dirt road. They passed an oil lease and saw the "rocking horse" dipping back and forth like some giant bird feeding.

"Is that one of ours?" Yokomoto asked.

Bolan glanced down at the map in his lap, then nodded. "Third on the list. We start farther north. Almost on the Kansas line."

Yokomoto made two more turns, then pulled across a cattle guard, drove behind a thicket of blackjack oaks and spun the pickup back to face the road. "The others will be here shortly," he said.

They were the last words of his life.

Without warning, Bolan twisted in the seat and drove a hard right cross into the terrorist's jaw. The force of the blow knocked the man up against the driver's-side window.

The Executioner reached out and dug his hand into the soft flesh of Yokomoto's throat. Thumb and fingers encircled the windpipe, squeezed and pulled. A popping sound echoed off the walls of the enclosed cab as the Japanese's windpipe snapped in two. Yokomoto's arms and legs flailed uncontrollably, then he slumped back against the seat.

Bolan straightened the man up, then reached under Yokomoto's jacket and found a Ruger SP-101 in the shoulder holster. Digging through the terrorist's pockets, he found four speed-loaders filled with .357 hollowpoints.

The wheel gun was hardly his Desert Eagle or Beretta 93-R. But it would get him started.

The Executioner shoved the revolver into the back of his pants and stepped out of the vehicle as another pickup pulled behind the trees. He nodded, then motioned for the driver to circle and park next to where Yokomoto sat, staring open-eyed at the windshield. Walking casually toward the other pickup, Bolan waited for the man on the passenger side to roll down his window, then drew the Ruger from behind his back.

Jamming the gun inside the pickup to muffle the sound, Bolan fired.

The first round drilled through the skull of the passenger and into the shoulder of the driver. The passenger moaned softly; the driver shrieked.

The Executioner's second and third bullets ended the shriek. A fourth choked off the moan.

Bolan dumped the remaining two rounds with the empty brass, dropped a speed-loader into the weapon, then let it fall to the ground as he swung the cylinder shut again. He straightened both men in their seats, then dug through their clothing, coming up with a 13-shot Star Megastar .45 and a Glock 21. He dropped the revolver into his pants pocket, shoved the Megastar into his belt where the Ruger had been before and held the Glock behind the back of his leg at arm's length.

Thirty seconds later, a burgundy-and-silver Chevrolet pickup appeared from the road. The Executioner waved it around next to the other two trucks, then walked forward.

Again, the man in the passenger's seat thought there was something Bolan wanted to say to him. He rolled down his window.

The Executioner let the Glock speak for him. The look of astonishment on the passenger's face turned to terror as Bolan jammed the .45 into his temple and splattered brains and blood over the cab of the truck. The driver, a dark-skinned man Bolan had guessed to be Iranian at the house, fumbled at his belt.

The warrior squeezed the trigger again and the Glock's crisp "safe action" sent another round drilling into the man's throat. Blood gushed forth as Bolan fired again, this time forming a third eye in the terrorist's forehead.

He repeated the process of searching the pickup after straightening the men in their seats. He added two more pistols—a Browning Hi-Power in .40-caliber Smith & Wesson and another Glock, this one 9 mm—to his belt.

But the easy part was over.

The fourth and fifth pickups arrived simultaneously as the Executioner was closing the driver's side door. They slowed, moving at a snail's pace as they came toward him.

Bolan held the Glock .45 behind his leg again as he walked forward. He stopped next to a gray Dodge Ram pickup and looked through the window to see Pierre LaFayette behind the wheel.

The Belgian squinted through the late-afternoon light at the pickups already parked. Bolan followed his line of sight and saw what had alarmed the man.

Something, probably a postmortem muscle contraction, had caused Rei Yokomoto's body to fall face first across the steering wheel of the Ford.

The Executioner turned back to see the squinting eyes widen, and LaFayette's hand holding his Browning.

Bolan dropped beneath the driver's window as an explosion sounded over his head. The glass in the window shattered, raining over him.

The Executioner rolled to one side. Angling the barrel toward where LaFayette was seated, he jammed the Glock against the pickup door and pulled the trigger as fast as he could. Six rounds drilled though the door. He then rose to one knee, extending the pistol blindly over the doorframe and cutting loose with a string of .45s into the passenger area. Another half-dozen rounds blew from the weapon, then the slide locked open, empty.

The warrior let the Glock fall from his hand and reached behind his back for the Megastar as rounds began to wing his way from the truck behind the Ram. Rolling under the pickup, he twisted beneath the chassis, then gripped the .45 in both hands and aimed between the rear tires.

A fast volley of gunfire exploded the windshield of the last pickup, but Bolan didn't let up. Emptying the rest of the Megastar into the flying glass, he drew the Browning .40 and belly-crawled from the rear of the vehicle.

Rising to his feet, he saw two more dead terrorists in the final pickup.

"Yokomoto! LaFayette! What is happening?" The Executioner heard Asal's voice coming from the walkie-talkie in the pickup behind him. He sprinted to the driver's side and ripped open the door to find both LaFayette and his rider riddled with bullet holes and slumped together in the middle of the seat.

"Yokomoto! Come in! LaFayette!" Asal cried again over the walkie-talkie.

The Executioner jerked the bodies out of the truck and jumped in. The engine was still running, and dirt and grass flew from beneath the tires as the pickup spun back toward the road.

Bolan took a deep breath, clearing his head and transferring from battle mode to strategic planning. Asal had heard the shots, that was clear enough from his radio transmission. But there was no way of knowing what he would do next.

He might keep coming toward the trees, guns ready. He might hide, regroup and wait.

He might even abandon the plan and run.

In any case, the Iraqi still had the maps that marked both the location of the wells and the routes the Istad Itar terrorists planned to use between them.

The Executioner threw the transmission into Drive. He had effectively ended the threat to the wells in the western part of the Oklahoma Panhandle. But getting the maps to Brognola's counterstrike teams was the only hope he had of stopping the fiery carnage in the state's other counties.

Bolan twisted the wheel as he passed over the cattle guard and raced back toward the highway. He had set a trap. Most of his quarry had walked into it. But the occupants of the van and the Bronco had heard the shots. They had smelled the bait and recognized it for what it was.

Trapping hadn't worked.

So hunting season was about to begin.

9

The sounds of gunfire from behind the trees thudded dully against the glass of the Blazer's windows as Iraj Asal and Willem Gerhardt led the van down the road.

Asal gripped the walkie-talkie in one hand and steered with the other as a blind rage rushed from his chest to his brain. "LaFayette? Yokomoto?" he yelled into the radio. When he received no answer, he dropped the instrument to the seat, doubled up his fist and rapped himself across the forehead in frustration.

Suddenly the gunfire stopped.

Asal dropped his hand back to the radio and looked into the rearview mirror. He remembered hitting himself only once, but several red welts covered his face. A tiny trickle of blood dribbled down from his lower lip where his own fist must have smashed the tender membrane against his teeth. The lip was already swelling.

Control, damn it. He had to get himself back under control.

The leader of Istad Itar rubbed his face as he neared the trees. Why hadn't he listened to his instincts? He had gotten a funny feeling about Pollock the moment he laid eyes on the man. So why had he gone ahead and used him? The answer was simple. In a fit of temper much like the one that threatened him now, he had killed Skeeter Bradburn, the man he had hired to work out the oil well routes. He had needed someone, and needed him fast. That need had affected his judgment.

Asal glanced across the seat to Gerhardt. The German had introduced Pollock, and now, although the man's face showed no emotion, the guilt in his soul was as transparent as the glass behind him. Why had he not seen *that* before, as well?

The terrorist leader turned back to the front as the Blazer skidded toward the cattle guard that led to the trees. His heart screamed at him to plunge behind the thick trunks and leaves, to find Pollock and kill him. But his brain threatened that this course of action, like the killing of Skeeter Bradburn in his Amarillo office, would only complicate things further.

The Blazer ground to a halt.

"We must go see what has happened," Gerhardt said softly.

"No," Asal answered. "I know what has happened. It was your American, Pollock. He has killed them. He has killed them all."

Gerhardt turned toward him. "Be reasonable. One man has killed all the others? *No* man could do that. How can you know?"

"I know," Asal said. "This man is...special." He threw the Blazer into reverse and skidded back over the cattle guard. The walkie-talkie fell forward onto the floor.

As they started back down the road, Asal saw the van turn the corner a quarter mile away and start toward them. He found the walkie-talkie on the floor between his feet and lifted it to his lips. "Mohammed," he said quickly, "return to the highway immediately."

"What?"

"Do it!" Asal roared.

Dirt flew from beneath the Blazer's tires as Asal and Gerhardt sped forth to meet the van. The panel vehicle had backed onto a cow path as they sped by. "Follow us!" Asal shouted into the radio as he guided the Blazer over the ruts in the packed dirt.

He watched the rearview mirror until he turned the corner, then sat back against the seat. "We must alert the other teams," he said out loud. "There might be other men like Pollock ready to strike."

They reached the highway a few minutes later and the Blazer led the van onto the two-lane, then north toward the Colorado border. Asal closed his eyes, fighting the fury that still threatened to overtake him. The simplicity of the oil-field strike had been its strong point. The real power, the central command if you would, had remained in Baghdad with Saddam. Asal had been given loose control over all of the teams once they'd reached the U.S., but the plan had been intact before they left Iraq. With the exception of working out the best paths between wells, there had been little to do but wait for the appointed time and set the fires.

How could it have gone so wrong?

The terrorist struck himself across the face again and screamed. The Blazer and van crossed the Colo-

rado border and sped on as he caught himself and
slowly rubbed the new wound above his eye. *Control.*
One eye on the road, he rubbed the other until it
burned like the fires of hell.

At this point, there were only two things that could
be done. One of them was to contact the other team
leaders as quickly as possible, informing them of what
had happened. Pollock had been a demon sent from
the Great Satan, and where there was one devil, there
were likely to be more.

Asal finally dropped his hand to his lap and looked
up into the mirror. His eyes were bleeding now, small
trickles of blood dripping down to join the red that
came from his lip. Then, with the suddenness of a
lightning bolt striking, reality caught hold of the terrorist. He turned toward Gerhardt. "The oil fields
were merely a red herring, designed to keep the
Americans' attention occupied while another strike
was prepared," he said. "There is more, isn't there,
Willem?"

Gerhardt smiled. "Of course there is more, Iraj."

A green sign on the side of the road read Campo 45.
Asal cursed. The terrain was no longer flat as it had
been in Oklahoma. It was more like New Mexico, with
steep hills and twisting curves that kept speed down.
Even at the breakneck pace he was employing, it
would be more than half an hour before they reached
the town and found a telephone.

But was it even necessary now? "Should I proceed?" Asal asked. "Still try to contact the others?"

Gerhardt's face finally showed emotion. Surprise.
"Certainly. It would be nice if we were able to set fire

to the oil wells in addition to employing the real strike.''

''Tell me of the other strike,'' Asal said as they sped down the road. He turned toward the German and saw the man trying to decide.

Finally Gerhardt shrugged and began to talk. When he finished, Asal was practically cackling with joy. What had been planned as a second wave of terror for the United States was even greater than setting aflame the oil fields of Oklahoma. The knowledge thrilled him, and made him want *both* strikes to succeed.

Asal looked up at the sky. The sun was low on the horizon, ready to set. Then, like most of the decisions he made, the Iraqi made his next impulsively. Seeing a sprawling ranch-style house appear a half mile off the road in the distance, he slowed, then led the van onto a gravel drive toward the building. They would have a phone.

Asal raised the walkie-talkie again. ''Drive slowly,'' he ordered the van, ''as if we are lost and looking for directions.'' He paused. ''But when we reach the front, drive to the rear of the house and go in the back door. Do it quickly, and shoot anyone who tries to stop you.''

The terrorist slowed the Blazer further as they approached the house, then brought it to a halt ten feet from the low front porch. A five-year-old Lincoln Continental stood under a tree in the front yard. Two pickups—one a late-model Chevy, the other an aging Ford with welding equipment bolted to the bed—were parked close to the barn a hundred feet away.

"Get ready," Asal told Gerhardt. "We go as soon as the van rounds the back." He jerked Pollock's Desert Eagle from under his jacket, then turned to smile at the German. "Are you ready?" he asked.

Gerhardt nodded, returning the smile.

The van passed them and rounded the corner of the house as a middle-aged man wearing striped overalls and a long-sleeved shirt stepped out onto the porch, glancing at both vehicles.

Asal held the Desert Eagle behind his back as he got out of the car. He smiled at the man, then he pumped two raging .44 Magnums through the striped overalls.

The Iraqi led the way up the step and onto the porch, firing another round into the fallen farmer as he leaped over the body and crashed through the door. He found himself in a wood-paneled entryway that led to a kitchen on one side, a living room on the other.

Another crash came from the rear of the farmhouse as the men in the van shattered the back door. A scream echoed from the back of the house. Asal sprinted toward the sound, racing through the living room and down a short hallway. He ground to a halt outside a bathroom door where the men from the van stood aiming their weapons over the threshold.

The Istad Itar leader looked through the opening. A middle-aged woman with chestnut hair stood naked in the bathtub, her feet and ankles invisible in the soapy water below. She screamed again, trying to cover herself with her hands as Asal walked past the sink and stopped in front of her.

"Where is your phone?" he demanded.

The woman's answer was another scream.

Asal slapped her hard across the mouth, putting all of his frustration and disappointment behind the blow. "Gerhardt!" he shouted, turning around.

The German was nowhere to be seen.

Asal hit the woman again and she flew back against the wall, then slid down into the tub and sent sudsy water up to spray over the terrorist's face and clothes.

Shoving the Desert Eagle between the woman's heaving breasts, he shouted, "Where is your phone!"

The woman opened her mouth. Whether to scream again, or answer his question, Iraj Asal never knew.

For at that moment, it suddenly sounded as if the whole front of the house was caving in.

THE EXECUTIONER STOOD on the accelerator, skidding the Dodge Ram around the trees, over the cattle guard and back toward the highway.

A mile ahead, he saw the trail of dust on the county road. Flooring the foot feed again, he guided the pickup over the top of the washboard road, fighting the steering wheel with both hands each time a tire sank into one of the deep depressions and threatened to fishtail out of control.

His prey had decided to run, rather than fight. He wasn't surprised, but he was far from happy. The chase would take time, which he didn't have. The sun was setting, and before long the oil wells in Cimarron County might be the only ones left in the state of Oklahoma.

A mile later Bolan topped a hill. He could still see the tiny trails of dust in the distance. Just beyond them, the highway appeared. Then the hill sloped into a gully that crossed the road. The warrior guided the Ram along the road, the trails of dust disappearing under the horizon in the distance.

When he reached the crest of the next hill, the dust still remained in the air. But the tiny specks that had been ahead of it—the Blazer and the van—had disappeared.

Right or left? Bolan wondered as he slowed, sliding though the settling dirt storm like an airplane coasting through the clouds. North or south?

He didn't know and ground the pickup to a halt. His eyes searched southward first. The highway made a sharp bend, disappeared behind another of the maddening knolls that were just high enough to block his vision, then appeared again and crossed a trestle bridge a half mile away.

To the north the road rose steeply and straight.

The van and Blazer both had time to vanish behind either barrier. But unless the Executioner missed his guess, they didn't have time to cross the bridge.

Turning back to the south, Bolan waited. The seconds ticked away, feeling like minutes and then hours as he waited to see if the two vehicles would emerge onto the bridge. He forced himself to wait sixty seconds—twice as much time as he guessed it would have taken the men to round the hill and appear again, then twisted the steering wheel to the right and started north.

The terrain changed slightly as he crossed the state line into Colorado. He mounted hill after hill, then dropped down into the shallow canyons that divided them. Each time he topped one of the peaks, the Executioner's eyes strained down the highway, searching for the two vehicles. Each time, he saw nothing in the dwindling light.

The Ram raced past a green road sign. Campo 45. Bolan barely made out the words in the fading light. He switched on his headlights.

Campo, Colorado, forty-five miles away, was the next town. Would Asal take the chase that far? Bolan didn't think so. The terrorist leader would be as anxious to alert his own men as the Executioner was to contact his. Neither of them had time to eat up on forty-five miles of second-rate two-lane highway.

The warrior forced his foot to lighten on the accelerator. He scanned the roadsides now, searching for dust motes still floating through the dusk at each quarter-section road. He saw a junked car on top of a rise, and read the sign painted on the door as he sped past. Lillian's Lounge. Behind the sign, he saw an old trailer that had been converted into a roadside tavern.

Darkness was about to fall in earnest by the time the Executioner saw the one-story ranch house ahead. His foot rose automatically, slowing the pickup again as his eyes strained in his head. Two shadowy specks were moving down the drive to the house.

As they passed under a tall yard light, Bolan saw both the Blazer and the van.

The Blazer came to a halt in front of the house. The van continued around the side as someone stepped out onto the porch. Two figures—Asal and Gerhardt, he assumed—exited the Blazer. A second later, the shadowy figure on the porch fell to the ground.

The Executioner turned into the drive as one of the men from the Blazer raced up the step to the porch. The other hesitated, then sprinted toward the rear of the house.

Loose gravel shot from beneath his wheels as Bolan curved along the path. Still straining his vision, he saw a clump of stripes lying outside the front door under the porch light.

Bolan knew what he had to do. With one hand, he snapped the seat belt around his waist. Asal hadn't hesitated to gun down the man on the front porch. The terrorist wouldn't delay any more in killing anyone who was inside the house.

Twisting the steering wheel, Bolan floored the accelerator again. The pickup's engine roared as the vehicle neared the house. Then the wheels struck the step, throwing the front of the vehicle high in the air. The tires came back to the ground just as the hood crashed through a large picture window.

Bolan hit the brakes, skidding to a halt almost against the wall on the other side of the living room. He snapped open the seat belt, and a split second later had opened the door and was diving out onto the floor.

Bolan drew the Browning automatic from his belt and rolled to his belly. He heard excited voices down a hallway that led to the back of the house. Footsteps pounded his way, and a second later, one of the terrorists he remembered from the farmhouse emerged into the living room.

The Executioner fired twice, hammering both rounds into a spot the size of a quarter in the man's chest. Before the terrorist could hit the ground, Bolan had leaped to his feet and was racing past him into the hall.

Two more men stood there, dumbfounded, their AK-47s aimed at the ground. Their confusion didn't last long however, and as the third .40-caliber round left the barrel of the Browning the Russian weapons began spitting gunfire.

Bolan took to the floor once more, pumping the trigger as he fell. A lightning-fast volley of semiauto fire leaped from the barrel of the Browning, drilling into the men and driving them back down the hall. One fell to the floor, but the other stayed upright. But not for long.

The warrior fired again, opening a hole the size of a golf ball in the front of the man's skull. The terrorist toppled forward on top of his comrade.

The Executioner heard noise farther down the hall and got to his feet. He lifted one of the AK-47s from the hands of a dead man, shoved the Browning back into his belt, then stopped just short of a door that led off the hall. Peering cautiously around the corner, Bolan saw a nude woman sitting in the bathtub. Her face was frozen in shock.

Creeping silently past the doorway and on down the hall, Bolan stopped and glanced into a bedroom. Empty. Another bedroom was equally unoccupied, and he stopped again at a corner that turned toward the backyard.

Quiet, almost imperceptible breathing came from just around the corner.

The Executioner stepped back and aimed chest-level through the plasterboard corner at the spot from which the breathing had come. His finger tightened on the trigger, then stopped.

He had no idea whose breath it was just inches away. It might be Asal or one of his men. But it might just as easily be another member of the unlucky farm family whose lives would never be the same after tonight.

If any of them *had* lives after tonight.

Dropping to one knee, Bolan moved away from the corner until his back made contact with the opposite wall. For what he had in mind, the rifle would be too unwieldy, and he quietly placed it on the hardwood floor. Drawing the Browning once more, he took a deep breath, then fell prone into the opening.

Automatic gunfire blew over the Executioner, striking the plaster wall and sending a storm of white powder swirling into the hall. Bolan's vision picked up four blurry forms as he hit the floor.

Two men stood side by side in the hallway, holding AK-47s.

The warrior tapped the trigger once for each man, catching the first in the *X* ring in his chest, the second in the throat. They fell to the floor as Bolan swung the Browning to the side, then suddenly stopped.

Khalid was the man's name. Bolan remembered him from the deserted farmhouse. He stood now in the hallway, facing the Executioner. One caterpillarlike eyebrow grew over the dark beady eyes that sank deep into his skull, and the smile on his face was that of a poker player holding a full house, aces high and kings low.

Instead of cards, he held a young woman of nineteen or twenty.

The Arab's arm was wrapped around the woman's neck, his pistol shoved against her temple. The scene was almost an instant replay of the situation the Executioner had found himself in the day before.

But "almost" was the operative word. There were two big exceptions. Bolan was on his side, aiming up, with a far worse angle of trajectory than he'd had at the Jim Thorpe building.

And the look of terror in the young woman's eyes told him she was no Paula Kiethley. She was in shock. Not only could the Executioner not count on this girl's help in her own rescue, she might well come out of the semicoma she was now in at any moment. If she did, she'd likely panic and get in the way.

"Drop your weapon!" Khalid yelled.

Bolan lined the sights up on the eyebrow.

The terrorist saw what he was doing and ducked lower behind his hostage, spoiling his aim. "Drop it!" he repeated.

The warrior didn't move. "I don't think so."

"What?"

"I said I don't see any future in dropping my gun," Bolan replied. "You'd just kill me, then I wouldn't get a chance to kill you."

"I will kill *her!* Then you!"

The Executioner had resigned himself to death more years ago than he could remember, and now, as he looked into the comatose eyes of the innocent young woman, he would have gladly given up his own life to save hers.

But that wasn't the way it would work. If he dropped the Browning, Khalid's first round would take him out. The second bullet would kill the girl. Or it might work in reverse. It made little difference; the result would be the same.

Bolan knew he had one chance, and one only. It hinged on the fact that the man holding the gun didn't know much about him; certainly didn't know his code, or the rules that he imposed upon himself and would follow until death.

"Go ahead and kill her," the warrior said calmly. "I've never seen her before in my life and saving her isn't my job. I'm here to stop the wells from going up." He paused for a second to let his words sink in. Surprised, the Arab's face strained unconsciously forward to hear more, higher over the girl's shoulder. The furry eyebrow became visible, then the eyes beneath it.

"Fact is," Bolan went on. "if you don't hurry up and kill her, I'll have to do it myself. She's getting in my way, keeping me from doing my job." He held the Browning steady. The sights were once again on a spot just below the terrorist's nose, and the juncture where the two eyebrows became one. But the angle was still bad. He had less than half an inch clearance over the young woman's shoulder, and less than that to the side of her cheek.

The confidence had drained completely from Khalid's face. The man's eyes flickered right, then left, as if he might be hoping one of the men on the ground would rise from the dead and come to his aid.

It was now or never. Bolan squeezed the trigger.

The single eyebrow divided as the terrorist's forehead caved in. The man took a step backward, dropped the gun and collapsed to the floor.

The Executioner rose to his feet. The young woman stood frozen in the same position she had when Khalid held her. When Bolan touched her, she didn't move.

From the front of the house, the Executioner heard the familiar sound of the Blazer kicking over.

Asal. Gerhardt. One of them, or maybe both. And the Iraqi still had the maps.

"Gerhardt!" Bolan yelled as he guided the petrified young woman into a bedroom and placed her gently on the bed. "Gerhardt?" When he got no answer, he sprinted through the rooms one by one, ending in the bathroom where the farmer's wife still sat in silence.

The Executioner slapped her lightly across the face. She looked up.

"You've got to come out of it," he told her.

The woman's eyes stared blankly.

Bolan slapped her again. "You daughter needs you. Your *daughter*."

The woman's eyes cleared. "Amy?"

"Amy needs your help. *Now*."

The Executioner helped her out of the tub and into a bathrobe that hung on a hook in the wall, then down the hall to the bedroom. The younger woman lay in a fetal position on the bed. "Call the sheriff," Bolan said, lifting the phone from the bed stand and shoving it into the woman's hand.

"My...husband..."

"Just call the sheriff," the warrior repeated. "And stay in this room until he gets here. Do you understand?

The woman nodded slowly.

Bolan waited for her to start punching in the numbers before he raced from the room, out the back of the house and to the van.

IN THE TWILIGHT, the Executioner could see the black Chevy Blazer at the end of the driveway as he pulled the van around the side of the house. He trod hard on the accelerator, but the van had little to give. As a pursuit vehicle, it was a washout.

Bolan glanced back toward the shattered picture window in the farmhouse. Steam had hissed from the radiator of the Dodge Ram as it came to rest in the living room a few minutes earlier, and he knew there was no point checking to see if it still ran. If it did, it wouldn't for long. And while he'd seen two more pickups and a Lincoln parked at the farm, he had no time to waste either hot-wiring the vehicles or searching for keys.

That left the van. And now, as it failed to respond to the pressure he exerted on the accelerator, jerking sluggishly forward and proving it would be no match for the Blazer, he wondered if his decision to forgo the farm vehicles might not have been in error.

The Blazer turned right onto the highway, heading north once more. Bolan followed, waiting until he hit the highway to flip on his own headlights. A half mile ahead, he saw the Blazer picking up speed.

Two cars passed going south before the Executioner slammed the steering wheel with both hands. It was an uncustomary exhibition of frustration on his part, and it passed quickly. Anger would get him nowhere. Calm, controlled and rational thinking would. There might still be a chance to overtake Asal and get the vital information to Brognola before it was too late.

But as he watched himself continue to drop farther behind, finally losing sight of the Blazer altogether, the warrior had no idea what that chance would be. He had no other choice but to pursue as quickly as the van allowed, and hope an unforeseen opportunity of some kind presented itself before it was too late.

More cars passed them going south as they ate up the miles. Darkness finally fell for good over what had now become flatland. Bolan knew that by now the other nineteen teams of Istad Itar would be starting to make their way from hiding toward the first wells on their lists.

Soon, the state of Oklahoma would begin to look like Kuwait after the Gulf War.

A passing vehicle heading south suddenly screeched its tires. Bolan looked into the rearview mirror and saw a blue-and-white Colorado State Patrol car back across the highway and reverse directions. A radar gun hung out of the driver's-side window.

Bolan frowned as the vehicle's twirling red lights came on. The last thing he needed was more time wasted while the trooper wrote out a ticket. On the other hand, he might be able to turn this traffic stop into the break he needed.

The Executioner lifted his foot from the pedal and slowed. Pulling to the side of the road, he drew the Browning from the side of his waistband and hid it behind his back. In the side mirror, he watched the trooper replace the radio mike on his dash, then step cautiously out of the car.

The blue-uniformed man walked forward, his hand on the grips of the gun at his side. He stopped three feet to the rear of the window and said, "License and insurance verification please." His eyes never left the Executioner.

Bolan put as much nervousness and embarrassment into his voice as he could muster. "Yes, sir," he said. "Just one second..." Slowly he reached behind his back as if going for his wallet. But when his hand came around, it held the Browning .40-caliber automatic, cocked and locked. "Freeze!" he growled.

His hand still on the grips of his holstered gun, the trooper's expression didn't change. Only his eyes betrayed the decision he was about to make. A decision he knew might mean life or death.

It *was* a life-and-death decision, the warrior knew, but not in the way the trooper thought. Mack Bolan had always considered policemen his brothers, compatriots in the war against crime and evil. He had never shot one yet, and he didn't intend to do so now. If the trooper chose to draw and fire, Bolan wouldn't resist. He would die there on that dark road in Colorado near the Oklahoma border.

Slowly the trooper raised his hands above his head.

Bolan stepped out of the vehicle, unsnapped the thumb break on the trooper's holster and found himself holding a Beretta 92. He jerked two extra magazines from their holders, dropped them in his pocket and said, "Step over next to the van and turn around."

The trooper was around five-ten and a muscular two hundred pounds or so. "Fuck you. If you're gonna kill me, you're gonna do it looking at me."

Bolan stared at him. "I'm not planning to kill you unless I have to. But if you don't turn around, I *will* have to."

"No."

The Executioner knew more time was flying as he argued with the man. And besides that, he could already see in the trooper's eyes that the man regretted the decision to give up his gun. Any second now, he'd make a play for the Browning.

Bolan swung the gun hard against the trooper's jaw.

A loud crack echoed in the stillness of the night as the trooper slumped to his knees. The warrior stepped in quickly, jerking the handcuffs from the dazed man's belt pouch and cuffing him to the side mirror of the van. "Where are the keys?" he asked.

Anger filled the trooper's eyes as they began to clear. "Other pouch," he mumbled.

Bolan pulled out a key ring and saw both keys to the vehicle and the handcuffs.

Hurrying back to the car, the Executioner got in and started the engine. The trooper stood glaring at him on the side of the road.

Bolan threw the pursuit vehicle into drive and pulled up alongside the man.

The trooper stood his ground, staring in hatred. *"Now* is when you shoot me, huh, maggot?" he growled.

Bolan couldn't suppress a grin. The guy had guts. The Executioner had no intention of leaving him weaponless and helpless by the side of the road. Slipping the handcuff key off the ring, he leaned across the seat and handed it to the trooper. The man took it, his eyes opening wide in surprise.

He was even more surprised when Bolan dropped the magazine from the Browning, worked the slide to empty the chamber, then replaced the round in the partially spent mag. Aiming the trooper's own gun through the window, he said, "Sorry, but I need the extra magazines that fit your Beretta. The Browning has about half a load left in case you run into any trouble. I'll drop it out the window as I drive off. Watch where it lands."

Before the trooper could answer, he drove forward, threw the gun onto the grass and sped off after Iraj Asal once more.

10

Radio traffic scratched from the police scanner on the dash as Bolan watched the handcuffed trooper grow smaller and then disappear in the rearview mirror.

The Executioner didn't kid himself. Asal would have been able to put several miles between them during the time he had been sidetracked with the Colorado State Patrolman. But it had been necessary. The van was never going to catch the Blazer. The high-performance engine inside the blue-and-white Chevrolet, designed for just such high-speed pursuits, had a chance.

Bolan glanced down at the speedometer, seeing the needle pass the 100-mile-per-hour mark, then move to 120. Lights outside the scattered farmhouses flashed by. The land was mostly flat, but he navigated the occasional curve with the skill of a Formula One race car driver.

There was another problem besides the fact that Asal had such a big head start. The man didn't have to go to Campo. He might decide to stop and commandeer the phone at another farmhouse.

The Executioner's hand moved to the controls on the dash, searching for those that operated the spotlight mounted just outside the window. He swept the beam across the houses, barns, and yards as he passed. The bright light illuminated the areas well—from the front. But if Asal had parked the Blazer inside one of the barns, behind one of the houses, or if he'd taken one of the dirt roads leading away from the highway and gone looking for a more remote house...

Bolan shoved the destructive thoughts from his mind. If that happened, there was nothing he could do. It wouldn't help to dwell on it. But somehow, his instinct told him Asal wouldn't stop at another house.

The warrior had known countless criminals over the years, and they all fell into one of two categories: those who performed alone, and those who needed "the pack." Iraj Asal struck Bolan as a man who might show courage when protected by other guns, but whose tail fell immediately between his legs when alone.

Even with his men, Asal had been unable to successfully take over the farmhouse several miles back, and Bolan felt certain that this time he would decide to slip quietly into Campo and use the nearest pay phone.

The patrol car raced on, passing slower moving traffic as the Executioner drew closer to the small southern Colorado town. He heard the Colorado State Patrol radio dispatcher attempting to contact unit 940, looked down at the push-button programmable radio in front of him and saw that the call numbers matched. But it hadn't been long since he had cuffed the trooper to the other vehicle, and the woman's voice betrayed no alarm. Bolan knew she would be thinking the trooper was outside the vehicle writing a ticket on the high-speeding van.

Bolan passed a sign announcing Campo, 13 Miles, then pulled in behind a blue Volvo that was observing the 55-mile-an-hour speed limit. He started to pass, then saw the string of headlights, coming his way. Switching on the red lights and siren, the warrior waited until the Volvo had pulled to the shoulder, then shot past.

Another two minutes and the pursuit car topped a high ridge. Perhaps a half mile ahead, under the glow of the moon, the Executioner saw a vehicle hurry over the top of another hill and disappear.

Bolan didn't deceive himself. It might be the black Blazer. It was the right size and general shape. But at that distance it might just as well be a Bronco, Jimmy, Jeep, or any of several other similar vehicles.

Leaning even harder on the foot feed, the Executioner forced the last ounces of power out of the screaming engine. The speedometer needle jumped to 140 and stopped, but the car continued to increase speed. Thick growths of trees flashed by on the side of the road, creating the illusion of a tunnel. When he emerged into the open once more, the Executioner found himself a hundred yards behind the black vehicle.

Which, he could see now, *was* a Blazer. But was it the right one? He still couldn't tell.

Bolan slowed slightly, gaining on the car ahead at a speed he hoped would draw no attention. The Blazer was doing at least eighty mph, and if it was Asal, he had no desire to alert the man of his presence.

Slowly the pursuit car drew in behind. By now the driver would have spotted the marked unit. Through the rear windshield, the Executioner could see an unidentifiable head above the front seat. He reached for the spotlight, then stopped, doubting that more illumination would tell him any more than he already knew. It would, however, warn Asal or whoever was driving the vehicle that he was under surveillance.

What told the Executioner more than any spot ever could, was the fact that the Blazer made no attempt to slow down. The natural instinct of generally law-abiding citizens who spotted a cop while speeding was to hit the brake. The Blazer maintained speed.

There was only one way to make sure.

Bolan gunned the engine, pulled into the oncoming lane and started to pass. As he did, headlights rounded a curve ahead and forced him back. A red Toyota raced past.

The Executioner decided on another course of action. Flipping the bar lights atop the vehicle, he waited until they flashed their red beams

The Blazer didn't slow.

Bolan hit the siren, and this time, the Blazer increased speed.

It had to be Asal.

The Executioner drew the trooper's Beretta from his belt and held it between his clenched knees. He pulled into the opposing lane again, but a roaring semi-trailer forced him back behind the Blazer. He waited for the truck to pass, then saw the long stream of headlights coming his way as they drew nearer to Campo.

Bolan fell in behind the Blazer once more, then leaned forward, flooring the accelerator. The patrol car shot forward like a rocket, ramming the back of the Blazer.

The driver's head snapped back.

The Executioner rammed the Blazer again, as he waited for the headlights to pass. When the last car flashed by, he pulled back into the passing lane and drew alongside the Blazer.

Asal turned toward him, squinting into the patrol car. His eyes focused on Bolan, his mouth opening in shock, his lips forming a silent "Pollock."

The warrior aimed the Beretta through the passenger's window and fired just as the Iraqi hit the brakes. The Blazer fell back, and the Executioner's shot went wild. Bolan stomped his own brake pedal and raised the gun again.

As he did, more headlights appeared ahead.

The tires beneath the patrol car squealed in agony as Bolan dropped behind the Blazer again, narrowly missing an oncoming Nissan. The driver leaned on his horn as he passed, but by then the Executioner was pulling out and up next to the Blazer once more.

Bolan fired a rapid volley of semiauto 9 mm rounds, missing Asal as the man veered off the road onto the shoulder. The slide on the Beretta locked open, empty. The Executioner dropped his speed, letting the Blazer take the lead once more. They topped a ridge, and the lights of the small town of Campo appeared, about four miles ahead.

The warrior dropped the Beretta on the seat next to him and looked down at the Remington 870 shotgun riding vertically in the locked rack next to the radio. The key to the lock would be on the key ring—in the ignition. His fingers found the key as he sped along the road, slowly working it off the ring as he guided the vehicle with one hand. Unlocking the rack, he pulled the shotgun out and placed it on the front seat beside him.

A grim look of determination covered the Executioner's face as he rested the wooden stock against his thigh, then racked the slide with one hand to chamber a 12-gauge shell.

The lights in the distance had grown brighter, and Bolan knew he had to act quickly. If Asal made it into Campo, innocent citizens could be put at risk. A wreck might take out pedestrians, not to mention the fact that anyone on the street would become a potential hostage.

Changing hands on the steering wheel, Bolan extended the shotgun out the window and rested the barrel on the hood. He leaned out quickly, dropping the front bead sight on the Blazer's left rear tire. Flame leaped from the barrel as the blast of 12-gauge shot skidded over the patrol car's hood and into the tire.

When the tire blew, the Blazer skidded into the oncoming lane, turned sideways, then backward, and continued backward down the highway.

Bolan jammed the stock against his shoulder, reached out with his left hand and grabbed the slide. Racking another shell into the chamber, he raised his aim and fired again. The second round was a slug that drilled through the windshield, leaving a tight hole the size of a baby's fist.

The Blazer spun back across the pavement, slipped into the ditch, then turned over. Bolan slowed as the vehicle continued to roll though a barbed-wire fence and into a grassy pasture, finally coming to rest upside down against a water trough.

The Executioner slammed on the brakes as he guided the patrol car down into the ditch and up the other side. He stopped just short of the downed fence posts, leaped from the vehicle and sprinted toward the Blazer.

Soft moans came from the overturned vehicle as Bolan stopped next to it. He worked the slide once more, racking another shell into the ready position. Holding the Remington under his arm, he leaned down and grabbed the door handle.

The door came off in his hand. Just inside, he saw the pained face of Iraj Asal, blood streaming from a gash above his forehead, covering his eyes.

"Help...me..." the Iraqi moaned.

Bolan opened the rear door of the Blazer, dropped to his knees and crawled through. He found Asal's briefcase intact and resting on the overturned roof. The maps were inside. The warrior crawled back out of the Blazer and stood, looking down at the racked and mangled body before him.

"Doctor..." Asal pleaded. "Please...my leg is...I think it's broken."

"That's the least of your problems. Where's your German friend?" Bolan demanded.

Asal moaned. "Who?"

"Gerhardt. Where is he?"

The terrorist shook his head. "I don't know...
please...my leg...."

The Executioner reached down, dragged the man
from the car and jerked him to his feet. He screamed,
but stood steady.

"It's not broken," Bolan said. He shook the man
down quickly, finding the Desert Eagle still stuffed
inside the terrorist's belt. He found the Walther PPK
and Asal's dagger inside the overturned Blazer. Shoving the Desert Eagle into his own waistband, he
pushed the shotgun under Asal's chin. "I'm not going to ask you again. Where's Gerhardt?"

The Iraqi wiped blood from his eyes with his shirt-
sleeve. "I do not know. I have not seen him since the
farmhouse."

Bolan pushed the man to the patrol car and opened
the door to the back seat. "Get in."

A moment later, the Executioner had found another set of handcuffs in the glove compartment and
secured Asal on the floor.

Seconds later he was racing toward the lights of
Campo, Colorado, hoping he would still have time to
get the well locations to Brognola's counterstrike task
force before the state of Oklahoma went up in flames.

THE TIN-SIDED IGA grocery store was dark as Bolan
pulled into the parking lot and killed the lights in front
of the phone booth. "Keep your head down and your
mouth shut, and maybe you'll live," he told Asal over
the seat.

The terrorist remained silent.

Bolan grabbed the briefcase and glanced around him at the peaceful small-town setting as he got out— light traffic on the streets, an elderly couple walking, holding hands, a group of teenage boys on the porch of the house across the street, talking and laughing. None of them seemed to have noticed that the man driving the Colorado Highway Patrol car was dressed in dirty blue jeans. Or if they did, they didn't care.

The warrior dropped a quarter into the slot, gave the operator the number of the OSBI headquarters in Oklahoma City, told her to ask for the deputy director's office and reversed the charges.

"Will you accept charges on a call from Rance Pollock?" he heard the operator ask a few seconds later.

"Yes," Hal Brognola answered.

The operator hung up and Brognola said, "Striker? Where are you?"

"Campo, Colorado."

"What?"

"It's a long story that we don't have time for. But I've got the route maps."

"By now the terrorists must be nearly to the first wells. The fires are liable to start any second. You got a fax machine available?"

"No. For right now, let me read you the location of the first wells on the remaining nineteen lists. You can get the troops started that way."

"Nineteen? I thought there were twenty."

"You can forget about Asal's team. They're dead. All but Asal. And I've got him with me."

"What about Gerhardt?" Brognola asked.

"Don't know. He's missing."

When Brognola didn't answer, Bolan opened the briefcase and pulled out the first map. "I'm starting with Team One in Nowata County. It's on the Kansas border, north-northeast of Tulsa. The first well is a Sun Oil Company lease near Coody's Bluff at the northern tip of Oologah Lake." He went on to give the legal description of the site. "Okay, move west to Osage County for Team Two," Bolan went on. "Just south of Fairfax." The Executioner continued until he had given the Justice man the first-strike wells for the remaining Istad Itar teams.

"We've got our forces in the air all over the state," Brognola said. "There should be someone reasonably close to all of those sites. I'll get on it. Hang on, let me see if we can find a place in Campo that has a fax."

Bolan heard the rustling of pages on the other end. "There's one in the Lanford Print Shop on Main Street." He gave Bolan the OSBI fax number, then said, "Get it to us quick, Striker. If we miss any of the first wells, we'll have to cut our losses and try to head them off before they get to the second."

"I'm on my way now, Hal. But one other thing. As soon as I leave the print shop, I'll be heading back across the state line to join the fight. The well site I'm nearest is close to Surrey Hills. Alert whoever's heading that way that I'm coming, give them my description and give me a frequency I can program into the radio in my unit."

"Your *unit?*"

"I'm driving a Colorado Highway Patrol car."

Brognola paused for a moment, then said, "Don't tell me. I don't want to know." He read a set of numbers, then both men hung up.

Sprinting back to the car, Bolan entered the frequency into the radio as he drove slowly down the street. The Lanford Print Shop stood in the middle of the block downtown. He drove to the corner, then cut down the alley and came to a halt behind a blue steel door. The Executioner pulled Asal from the back seat.

"My leg!" the terrorist complained again.

"Forget the leg."

The Executioner found a pry bar in the trunk of the patrol car. A moment later, the steel door stood open and he shoved Asal ahead of him into the dark shop. Moving through a workroom that smelled of ink, oil and disinfectants, he found the office near the front of the building.

The Arab sat next to the desk while the fax warmed up. Ten minutes later, copies of the routes the terrorists would be taking were in Brognola's hands.

But the work of the Executioner was far from over.

Throwing Asal into the back seat once more, Bolan reversed out of the alley.

"Where are we going?"

"For a drive," Bolan replied. "And on the way, we're going to have a little talk."

Asal hesitated. "About what?"

"About the fact that it seems to me that this has all gone a little too easy."

The silence from the back seat was loud enough to burst eardrums.

"There's more to this than just the wells, isn't there, Asal?"

"I do not know what you are talking about."

Bolan turned onto Highway 51 and headed west. "I think you do," he said. "Oh, I don't mean that you wouldn't have liked to set Oklahoma on fire. But that wasn't the real mission, was it? There's more. The wells were to keep us busy while something else went down."

Again, he got no answer.

"Start talking, Asal."

After another long pause, the Arab said, "And if I refuse?"

The Executioner glanced up into the rearview mirror.

"You did not answer me," the terrorist said from the floor of the back seat. "If I refuse to tell you about the second phase, you will kill me, I suppose?"

"No," Bolan replied calmly. "I won't kill you." He paused to let what he was about to say next sink in. "But when I'm done doing what I *will* do, you'll be begging me to."

THE FIRST SOFT, clipping sounds of distant helicopters sounded in the sky as the Executioner guided the patrol car off the highway onto a county road. He tapped the brake, slowing as he stuck his head out the window and looked up.

Moments later the shadows of three unlighted choppers crossed the moon.

Bolan pulled the radio mike from the dash and thumbed the button. "Justice 1242," he said, making up the call number on the spot. "Come in, Justice Task Force."

"Captain Yearick here," a low, gravelly voice crackled over the airwaves. "Come in 1242. You the guy Brognola told us would be at the party?"

"That's affirmative. I'm in a blue-and-white and heading toward the gate. Meet you on the ground."

"You got it, 1242. We've already dropped ground forces a quarter mile back. They should be close to position. The rest of us will repel."

"See you at ground zero," Bolan said.

"Let's get ready to rumble," Yearick came back, then clicked off.

The Executioner replaced the mike and switched on the overhead light. He glanced to the grid map of Texas County, Oklahoma, he had fastened to the trooper's clipboard mounted above the radio. Killing the light as quickly as he'd seen what he needed to, he switched the headlights off as well and guided the vehicle down the dirt road by the light of the moon. At the mile line he turned right, drove another mile, then made a left.

According to the map, the lease was half a mile distant. The entrance would be found on the north side of the road.

Earlier, the Executioner had stopped along the road long enough to remove the bar light from the top of the patrol car. The Colorado State emblems on the side doors wouldn't be visible until he got closer. At least he hoped they wouldn't.

As it turned out, it didn't matter.

The sounds of gunfire came suddenly from both the lease site and the air above it. Bolan stomped the accelerator and barreled down the road. As he neared, he slowed and saw a pathway that led off the road onto the lease. A pickup, facing the gate, was parked in the middle of the path next to the sign.

The Istad Itar backup truck. Assuming Team Fourteen was using the same plan as Asal's men, the second truck would stay on the road, its driver acting as a lookout and covering the rear while the primary pickup went onto the lease to start the fire.

"What am *I* supposed to do?" Asal whined from the back seat floor.

"Keep your head down," Bolan ordered. "If you're lucky, maybe it won't get shot off." He glanced over the seat. He had used Asal's own dagger to cut through the back seat, then cuffed the terrorist to the springs below. Asal wouldn't be going anywhere.

The helicopters could still be heard, hovering over an area where Bolan assumed the well had to be. He gunned the engine and shot forward down the road. The shadowy forms of men, standing in front of the pickup and to the sides, appeared in the darkness as he neared. They all held rifles, but aimed away from the road toward the direction from which the shots were coming.

A hundred feet from the lease entrance, the Executioner hit the brake. The patrol car skidded to a halt directly behind the pickup, the barrel of the Remington 12-gauge already extended through the window.

One man stood in the bed of the pickup. Resting his AK-47 over the top of the cab, he leaned over the roof toward the gate. As he heard the car behind him, he started to turn.

He didn't quite make it.

The Colorado trooper had alternated the shotgun magazine with double-aught buckshot and slugs. Bolan had replaced the slugs with more buckshot he found in the glove compartment, and as he squeezed the trigger now, a load of "dimes" blew from the barrel and shredded into the terrorist's chest.

The man sprawled out facedown in the truckbed as the other shadowy forms around the lease gate turned toward the patrol car.

The Executioner threw open the door and dived from the vehicle, pumping the shotgun and firing again as he hit the ground. A short stocky shadow fell to the dark road in front of the gate.

Bolan rose to his knees, pumped and fired again. Flames danced from the eighteen-inch shotgun barrel, as the buckshot sent a taller shadow tumbling to the ground.

Pump, fire, pump, fire, and two more dark specters fell to join their comrades.

Volleys of automatic 7.62 mm bullets blew toward the Executioner as he dived back to the ground and rolled toward the pickup. Coming up on his feet, he twisted as he jumped onto the bed, firing another load of buck into a silhouette only three feet from the rail of the truckbed.

A scream pierced the roar of the shotgun as Bolan fell on top of the body in the pickup bed. The terrorist next to the vehicle slumped below the tire wells and out of sight.

The warrior rolled to a sitting position on the dead man's back, swung the shotgun toward the surviving hardman and fired. The force of the blast blew the terrorist backward, an untidy heap leaking blood onto the ground.

The gunfire around the gate settled into an eerie silence, but autofire still crackled farther up the lease road. Bolan dropped the shotgun and tore the AK-47 from the hands of the corpse in the truckbed. He stuffed several extra magazines into his belt, then vaulted the side of the vehicle and hit the ground. Sliding into the cab, he found the keys still in the ignition. He fired up the engine and the pickup burst forward through the open gate.

The lease road angled upward, winding through several curves and past rows of trees that hid the well lease proper. The ever-increasing battle sounds told Bolan the firefight was close—just over a short rise. Slamming on the brakes, he exited the truck.

The Executioner hesitated briefly, turning to look at the body in the back of the pickup. Beneath it, the RPG-7 rested inside a pine crate. With the grenade launcher, and a little luck, he could take out half of the remaining Istad Itar terrorists with one shot.

With bad luck, he'd also kill half the counterterrorist task force. It was possible that the RPG-7 would strike the wellhead and set off an explosion that would take out the whole lease and everybody on it.

Bolan turned back toward the well area and sprinted to the top of the rise. Flames—muzzle-flashes— winked in the near distance. Hitting the ground near the top of the hill, he belly-crawled forward and looked down at the battle raging below.

A bulldozer had been parked to one side of the tank area. Stacks of pipe, bits, and even sacks of drilling mud scattered the area around the storage shed known in the oil fields as the "doghouse."

The task force had already rappeled from the helicopters. They had reached the ground and taken cover behind a number of shining white storage tanks near the well area.

Most of the terrorists had fallen behind the vertical tanks and separator. Bolan could see their backs in the moonlight. He counted eight.

Sporadic gunfire continued as men on both sides risked quick shots around the edges of the tanks. Both sides were being careful, doing their best to avoid hitting equipment that might suddenly turn the whole lease area into a fiery inferno. Bolan's gaze shot to the wellhead. No one was near it.

The Executioner turned back to the battle. Most of the terrorists exchanging fire with the task force were exposed, relying on the backup truck to cover their rear. He had a clear shot at most of them.

Bolan flipped the AK-47 selector switch to semiauto and sighted in on a hardman behind the gas meter. He waited until one of the task force men angled around a storage tank and fired, then pulled the trigger.

The task force gunner's round covered the Executioner's shot. Bolan watched the man at the gas meter jerk forward, spasm, and knew the bullet had entered somewhere along the spinal cord. The terrorist fell to the sparse grass next to the meter. The Executioner swung the rifle toward an Istad Itar gunman behind the pump jack and waited for the next volley. Another 7.62 mm round threw the man forward against the steel. He rebounded back onto the ground.

Swinging quickly to a terrorist crouching behind a stack of pipe joints beside the tanks, Bolan drilled a round into the man, punching him into the dirt.

Catching the terrorists with their backs exposed had been a stroke of luck. But Lady Luck was a fickle lover, Bolan knew, and when she arrived, she never stayed long. Now, after giving the Executioner three quick and easy kills, the elusive lady deserted him.

A bearded man who had taken cover beside the doghouse suddenly looked at the top of the rise, saw the Executioner and shouted a warning in Arabic.

The remaining five hardmen turned to look up the hill. Autofire chattered Bolan's way, forcing his head to the dirt. When he looked back up, he saw the terrorists racing for better cover.

Two of them died on the way. Bolan raised the AK-47 and felled the bearded man as he dived toward the rear of the doghouse. Another terrorist, trying to make his way to the side of a tank, took a slug from the M-16 of some unseen member of the task force.

But one hardman made it to the doghouse, leaping over the body of the man the Executioner had downed. Another raced away from the lease, through a volley of gunfire, squirming under the wheels of the bulldozer. The third man dived behind the stacked sacks of drilling mud, followed by a burst from an M-

16 that drilled into the sacks but fell short of the target.

Bolan waited until the rounds faded once more, then shoved a fresh magazine into the AK-47 and crawled on elbows and knees down the hill on a slow, roundabout course.

The Executioner could possibly face fire on two fronts, now. Yearick and the other members of the task force wouldn't be able to tell him from the terrorists. And if they spotted him, a bullet from "friendly fire" would kill as quickly as one from the terrorists.

The warrior spotted a grove of scrub oaks twenty feet behind the doghouse and angled that way as intermittent firing resumed. Reaching the thicket, he crawled under the gnarled bows and looked out to the small steel building.

Instead of one man, Bolan was surprised to see two. Both faced away from him, one at each corner of the building.

Two easy shots. But if he took them, the gunfire would give up his position to both the man behind the drilling mud and the other beneath the bulldozer.

Placing the rifle gently on the ground, the Executioner drew the dagger from his belt. He crawled forward out of the trees, staying low as he made his way toward the men at the rear of the doghouse. The next few seconds were crucial. He was still out of knife range, and if either of the two terrorists chanced to turn around...

Ten seconds later, Bolan was behind the men. Rising to his feet, he slid in, closing the gap, and raised the dagger high over his head in an ice-pick grip. His arm was on its way down when both men turned around.

The warrior lashed out with his foot, catching the nearer man in the groin. A muffled groan escaped from the terrorist's lips and he bent forward at the waist, the AK-47 falling from his grasp as he grabbed his crotch.

At the same time, the Executioner plunged the dagger past the other man's breastbone, twisting blade as it penetrated deep into the heart.

Bolan jerked hard, pulling the dagger free, and turned toward the man he had kicked, who was bringing his rifle in to target acquisition.

The Executioner drove the blade of the dagger into the terrorist's neck at the base of the spine and grabbed the man's rifle as he hit the ground. The warrior checked the magazine and chamber, then slung the weapon over his shoulder.

He turned toward the bulldozer. Moonlight reflected off the yellow steel, but the shadows beneath the vehicle concealed the hiding man. And the terrorist was no fool—he had no desire to reveal his position and hadn't fired since diving beneath the piece of heavy equipment.

That needed to change.

Bolan knelt next to the two bodies, ripped the long laces from the corpses' combat boots, then crept back into the trees. He retrieved the other AK-47 from hiding, set it on full-auto, wedged the barrel of the weapon between a fork in one of the branches and aimed it toward the bottom of the bulldozer.

As sporadic fire continued around the lease, the Executioner tied the bootlaces together, linked them to the rifle's trigger, then crawled away from the scrub oaks, letting the cord play out behind him.

The warrior gripped the second assault rifle in his right hand and aimed beneath the dozer. Holding the cord in his right, he jerked.

A volley of autofire shot from the treed rifle toward the bulldozer, drawing immediate return fire.

Bolan squeezed the trigger, aiming at the muzzle-flash beneath the heavy earthmover.

The return fire halted.

The Executioner heard whispering voices from behind the storage tanks and realized the task force had to have caught on to his presence. A quick prayer to the universe that they would remain silent rose to the heavens.

He was heard.

Bolan skirted the trees this time, belly-crawling toward the waist-high stack of drilling mud. The last terrorist had kept as low a profile as the man beneath the dozer, and the Executioner knew he might be anywhere on the other side of the stack.

Five feet from the mud, the warrior rose slowly and risked a quick look over the barrier. The man was low, somewhere on the other side. If the Executioner chose one of the corners, and it turned out to be the wrong one, he would emerge face-to-face with a rifle.

There was only one reasonable plan of attack, but taking it meant·exposing himself to the fire of the friendlies behind the storage tanks.

Bolan made the decision, rose to full height, then leaped onto the pile of drilling mud. One quick step took him to the other side as a short burst of 5.56 mm rounds fired from behind the tanks flew over his head.

"Hold your fire!" a hoarse voice screamed from across the lease as the warrior aimed down at the dirt.

The surviving hardman squatted facing outward. He twisted awkwardly, looking up into the face of his executioner.

Bolan's rounds drilled down through the top of his skull and into his brain. As the terrorist sprawled on the ground in a lifeless heap, the Executioner dropped flat on top of the mud sacks. The lease fell into silence.

"You Brognola's man?" Yearick's voice finally shouted.

Bolan smiled in the darkness. "More or less." He rose to his feet.

The counterstrike task force cautiously emerged from behind the storage tanks and walked forward.

A tall slender man stepped out of the shadows to face Bolan. He glanced at the bodies around the well site, then turned to his men. "Search the grounds. Make sure there aren't any more gunners hiding out."

The men spread out.

Yearick turned to Bolan. "I guess it's over."

Bolan thought of what Asal had told him during the drive from Colorado. As the Executioner had suspected for some time now, there was more to Saddam Hussein's attack on the U.S. than had initially met the eye. The well fires had been only the first step. He hadn't had time yet to interrogate Asal fully, and didn't know what phase two of the Istad Itar plan consisted of.

But he knew it was there.

Mack Bolan shook his head. "It's not over yet, Yearick. In fact, it's just beginning."

11

The elevator came to a stop on the third floor of the OSBI building. Grabbing the back of Asal's collar, Bolan almost lifted the terrorist from his feet as he followed Roy Wilson through a partially lighted waiting area to a door where the bearded agent was already entering a combination.

Wilson had met the task-force plane that had transferred Bolan and Asal from the oil well in the Oklahoma Panhandle back to Oklahoma City. Earlier in the evening, he had led one of the task-force units to a road near a well south of the city, where they had ambushed the Istad Itar terrorists before the hardmen even got close to the site.

The combination lock buzzed, then the door swung open. Wilson stepped back, holding it open for the other two men. He hurried around them and led the way down the hall.

Radio traffic crackled from an office in the corner of the building, and men—some in assault coveralls, others wearing traditional investigator business suits—came and went hurriedly through the doorway.

Bolan followed Wilson into the office, pushing the Iraqi terrorist in front of him. He saw Brognola, standing behind a large desk on which a radio base unit had been set up, talking to a broad-shouldered man in a camel-colored sport coat and brown slacks.

Oklahoma State Bureau of Investigation Deputy Director J. D. Baker had joined Brognola during co-ordination of the counterstrike effort, Roy Wilson had said. According to the agent, Baker was a personal friend from the days when both Wilson and the deputy director had been long-haired kids buying illicit drugs and kicking doors. Baker was out on a political limb this night, too, but like Wilson, willing to take any career chance necessary to keep the Oklahoma oil wells from going up in flames.

Bolan wondered. He knew he was likely to put the man's loyalty to the test. If Asal didn't start talking soon, the Executioner would have no choice but to start violating the "unconstitutional" rights that had been awarded to the predators of the world without regard for their victims.

The warrior pushed Asal in a chair in front of the desk as Brognola finished a radio transmission. He looked up at Baker. The man was in his mid-forties and wore a carefully trimmed mustache that matched his sandy-brown hair. Bolan glanced at the wall and saw several pictures of Baker on a racing bicycle. Others showed him shooting a revolver on a PPC course. The pictures told the warrior pretty much what he needed to know about Baker. The man was doing his best to stay active after being promoted to a paper-pushing job he probably hated.

The radio went silent. Bolan turned to Brognola. "The other sites?" he asked.

A weary smile curved the big Fed's lips. The un-lighted cigar stump in his mouth pointed toward the ceiling. "Got there in the nick of time on most of them. Two fires—one in Garfield County near Ga-bor, the other down in Love County along the Texas state line. Fire fighters are still there, but think they'll have them out in a few hours."

Bolan nodded. He glanced at an athletic-looking man in blue OSBI coveralls, standing against the wall. Brognola caught the Executioner's gaze and cleared his throat. He looked at Baker.

The deputy director nodded. "Scotty," he said, turning toward the agent, "things are dying down. Transfer command down to dispatch and take over."

The man turned and left the office.

Baker cleared the room of everyone except Bolan, Brognola, Wilson and Asal. He walked to the door and closed it.

The big Fed nodded to Bolan.

The Executioner moved in front of Asal and looked down at the handcuffed man. "We don't have much time, I'm guessing. I've suspected all along there might be a second phase to this assault. Gerhardt's been playing both ends against the middle. Now, I want to know exactly what else is about to go down."

Asal shook his head. "I do not know."

"Somehow, I don't believe you."

Since the battle at the well had ended, the terror-ist's confidence had been returning. Now, a cocky grin broke over his face. *"Somehow,"* he mimicked, "I do not *care."* His gaze roved over the room, and Bolan could see that he felt safe in the hands of the American criminal-justice system.

The Executioner glanced up at Baker.

The deputy director blew air through his lips in disgust, then said, "Give him one more chance."

Bolan turned back to Asal. "This is your 'one more chance.'"

The Iraqi shook his head. "I know nothing of this 'second phase' you speak of," he said, his sarcastic tone insuring that everyone in the room knew he was lying. "And if I did, I would not tell you. And I would like to remind you that I have certain rights. Including that of having an attorney present. I want one *now*."

Baker looked at Brognola, then Bolan. "He's right, you know." Slowly he moved around the desk to Bolan's side and looked down at the leader of Istad Itar. "You know, guy, we cops lived through the Miranda decision. Didn't like it, and knew it was hurting the good people and helping the bad, but we just sucked it up and went on and did our best. Then we lived through Esposito, then a dozen other bullshit court decisions." He paused, leaned down and placed both hands on the arms of Asal's chair. "But I've got a feeling that whatever this second part is that's coming, it might be even worse than your oil-well plan. So I've made a court ruling of my own."

With speed that belied his size, the OSBI man drew back a fist and drove it into the terrorist's nose.

Blood spurted from Asal's nostrils as the chair flipped over. The Iraqi landed on his back, his feet flailing the air.

Baker stepped forward, placing a foot on each side of the man's chest. Looking down, he said, "You have the right to remain silent. But if you do, you're gonna bleed like a stuck pig before I'm through with you. And when I get tired, I'm gonna let everybody else in this room who doesn't believe that terrorists have the right to kill innocent people take their shot at you."

Asal moaned.

The deputy director leaned down, gripped the front of the terrorist leader's shirt and hauled both man and chair back to a sitting position. His face an inch from Asal's, Baker went on. "You have the right to an attorney. And if there's anything left of you when we get finished, and we haven't decided to just dump your ass into one of the fires your men set, I'll think about getting you one." He paused to let it sink in.

"Do you understand these rights as I have stated them to you?" Baker asked.

Asal moaned again.

Baker drove another fist into the man's gut, then stepped back as the terrorist leaned forward, retching on the carpet.

"I asked you a question," Baker said when the vomiting had become dry heaves.

Asal nodded.

Baker drew back his fist and waited. "Then, do you wish to speak to me?"

The Istad Itar leader began talking, slowly, at first, his pace quickening as the effect of the punches began to wear off.

When he had finished, Bolan looked back at Hal Brognola and Roy Wilson. Their faces were ashen.

THE SOFT PURR of the North American Saber Liner's engines seemed to contradict both the somber atmosphere in the cabin and the gravity of the situation as Bolan, Brognola and Iraj Asal winged their way toward Washington, D.C.

SCUD. A simple, if rather harsh sounding word, it had become synonymous with horror during the Gulf War. Missile after missile had been launched by Iraq at Israel and Saudi Arabia, a few even slipping past the U.S. Patriot Missile System to kill innocent civilians on the ground below. Due to the inaccuracy of the design, and its medium-size warhead, the SCUD had been a weapon of terror rather than mass destruction.

Until now. According to Asal, Istad Itar had smuggled a SCUD into the United States. It was about to be launched at a target in the nation's capital.

And unlike those used in the Gulf, this SCUD was equipped with a chemical warhead that would spread the disease of anthrax up and down the eastern seaboard.

"Come in, Stony Man," the Executioner heard Brognola say. He turned toward the Justice man and saw the microphone in front of the G-man's face.

The voice of Aaron Kurtzman, the computer wizard of Stony Man Farm, a counterterrorist base out of which both Bolan and Brognola sometimes worked, came over the airwaves. "Sorry it took so long to get back to you, Hal," he said. "But here's what I came up with." He paused and cleared his throat. "Customs had no record of any suspicious imports from anywhere in the Mideast during the past sixty days.

But that didn't surprise me. This Istad Itar...with the contacts they've got, the components for both the missile and a mobile launcher could have come in from all over the world and then been assembled here."

"What about launching distance from Washington?" Brognola asked. "What kind of radius are we talking about?"

"They can shoot from anywhere within about a hundred and seventy-five miles of their target," he said.

Brognola's teeth clamped tight. He shook his head. "Transfer me to Barb."

"She's here with me now," Kurtzman came back.

A second later, Bolan heard the voice of Barbara Price, the mission controller at the Farm. "Go ahead, Hal."

"You heard back from the President yet?"

"That's affirmative. He wanted to stay at the Oval Office—said he had work to do and the chances of the SCUD actually hitting were about a million to one."

"You explained about the warhead?" Brognola queried.

"That's what got him out of there," Price said. "Navy HMX took him and the First Lady off a few minutes ago. They're on their way to Los Angeles on Air Force One."

Bolan smiled. There were two reasons he had wanted the President out of the White House and away from Washington. First, of course, he *was* the President. But the second reason was just as important. Unlike his predecessor, the new President had no military background or experience in covert operations. He tended to want to run the show, however, and the mission would function more efficiently with him out of the way.

"What about Federal Aviation?" Brognola asked.

"FAA called back just a minute ago," Price replied. "Their NOTAM area around the White House is usually one mile. They're extending it to ten, but that's as far as it's practical." Answering Brognola's remaining questions before he asked them, she said, "The Patriot missiles are being moved into the D.C. area right now. But it'll take time to set them up. In the meantime, the Air Force is already flying surveillance within the 175-mile radius, looking for anything suspicious."

Air surveillance was a good idea, and needed to be tried. But Bolan held little hope that the planes, or the recon satellites that were also being employed, would be of any help in the search for the small, easily camouflaged and highly mobile SCUD launcher.

They would have to find another way to locate the launch position. If they didn't, a SCUD missile loaded with a chemical warhead would explode in the capital.

Bolan sat back in his seat, closing his eyes as the plane began its descent. They were doing everything that could be done. But was it enough? The Patriots were a true stroke of genius, and had proved invaluable during the Gulf War. But they might not be operational by the time the SCUD hit the air. Even if they were, some of the missiles had slipped past the Patriots in the past. If that happened tonight, a lucky shot might take out the White House or nearby buildings of government. Even if they didn't, the anthrax warhead would spread disease to hundred of thousands, if not millions, of unsuspecting Americans.

Bolan looked down through the window and saw the lights of McCord Air Force Base. A few seconds later, the Saber Liner's wheels hit the runway and the plane glided to a halt.

The Executioner hurried down the steps to the ground.

He had won the fight for the oil fields of Oklahoma, but a brand-new battle was about to begin.

FROM HIS SEAT behind the pilot of the U.S. Air Force F-15 Eagle, Bolan examined the back of the man's head. In the early-morning light, it looked as if Jack Grimaldi needed a haircut. Wavy locks curled from under Grimaldi's helmet, poised to fall over the collar of his leather flight jacket.

The sight brought a smile to the Executioner's lips. Grimaldi might let the details of personal life, such as getting a haircut, slip by him once in a while, but such negligence never extended to his professional side. Grimaldi had been a top pilot in Vietnam, then become a close ally of Bolan's during the Executioner's years of war with the Mafia. It had seemed only proper that he be given the position of top pilot at Stony Man Farm when the counterterrorist installation came into existence, and he had been flying combat missions for Bolan and various squads who worked out of the Farm ever since.

Grimaldi had piloted everything from single-engine planes to the space shuttle. If it flew, he could fly it.

The plane reached three thousand feet and leveled off. Bolan activated the video screen. He would be acting as "alligator" during the surveillance flight, a slang term for the man behind the pilot who acted as a combination navigator, systems operator and weapons controller. Not that he planned on using the weapons with which the Eagle was equipped. The 20 mm M-61 gun and AIM-9 Sidewinders aboard had proved useful when launch sites had been located in the wide open deserts of southern Iraq, but it seemed far more likely that the SCUD near Washington would be hiding somewhere in a densely populated area, which precluded their use.

Bolan wrapped the headset around his ears and spoke into the mouthpiece. "You receiving, Jack?"

"Ten-four, Striker, loud and clear."

"Turn left, heading three-three-zero."

"You got it, big guy."

The plane veered slightly, then leveled off once more. Bolan watched the screen as familiar sites in and around Washington, D.C., appeared. The video was being linked immediately to a control center at McCord, and was also being viewed at the Pentagon. The Executioner knew that Brognola, as well as teams of surveillance specialists, were watching as closely as he was.

The warrior tapped a control button, switching to the radio ground unit. "Striker to McCord control," he said into the mike.

"Come in, Striker."

"Any word on the Patriots yet?"

"Still setting them up," the unseen voice came back.

"Not even an estimated time of operation?" Bolan asked.

"Not yet."

For a brief moment, an almost overwhelming feeling of futility threatened to come over the Executioner. What they were doing was looking for the proverbial needle in a haystack. The SCUDs and their launchers were small enough to hide in a million places within firing distance of Washington. Even if they weren't hidden outright, they could be camouflaged. The chances of the dozens of Air Force F-15 Eagles, or their Navy counterparts, the larger F-14 Tomcats, spotting anything suspicious were too miniscule to calculate.

Bolan concentrated on the screen. Okay, the chances were slim. But they'd be even slimmer if he talked himself into believing there was no chance at all.

The Eagle left the capital proper, then the District of Columbia. Bolan watched the screen as they passed over Maryland before entering the airspace of Pennsylvania. Below, he saw Johnstown and Altoona pass by. They continued on to the edge of the 175-mile SCUD range, altered course slightly and started back.

The Executioner closed his eyes for a moment, thinking. One of the largest searches in the history of the United States was going on below, with every police officer, National Guard and Reserve personnel, and even the regular military going over the countryside around Washington with a fine-tooth comb. But what were they looking for? A SCUD missile and mobile launcher—equipment small enough to be hidden in any barn, garage or similar building until a few minutes before launch time. Even when it was pulled out into the open, it would look similar to any flatbed truck and draw little attention until the missile was pointed toward the sky.

And by then, unless the Patriot system had been set up and was functioning, it would be too late.

WHEN HE'D BEEN a younger man, being trained by the infamous "Carlos the Jackal," Willem Gerhardt had learned to resent the term "terrorist." "We must use the weapon of terror, of course," Carlos had said. "But it is merely a means to an end."

Gerhardt had been taught that he was a "freedom fighter," battling not only for the oppressed souls in his home nation Germany, but for victims of the United States and allied nations the world over.

All bullshit, he knew now.

Over the years, the German had come to see that he was actually little more than a common criminal—a member of a gangster-style organization with self-interest and profit as the pinnacle goal. And he had come to learn an important thing about himself as a human being: he liked it that way. It made far more sense than the ridiculous notion that someday the peoples of the world would live together in harmony and equality.

Gerhardt stared down at the steak on the plate in front of him. The past few days had been a whirlwind of frantic activity, giving him little time to look at the overall picture. First, he had been given the okay to go ahead with his plan by Saddam Hussein. Then, he had made the anonymous phone call to Germany's GSG-

9 and informed them of the location of the safe-house. Then had come the battle with the MP-5-wielding counterterrorist squad, during which he had received an unplanned injury.

Gerhardt's left hand dropped to his knee as his right lifted his wineglass. It still hurt, but so what? The torn ligaments, tendons, whatever it was, could be repaired. And they were a small enough price to pay for what he was accomplishing.

After the safehouse, everything had fallen into place. Germany had turned him over to the U.S., where he had made sure that Rance Pollock kept busy searching for the oil-field strike sites. The oil wells had been the "sacrificial lamb" in Gerhardt's two-part strategy. It would have been nice if Oklahoma could have gone up in flames as well as the SCUD being launched on Washington, but it had never been expected that both strikes would be successful, and that wasn't how it had worked out.

Gerhardt took a sip of wine, then set his glass on the table. Yes, things had come off like clockwork. Oh, there had been a few anxious moments back in Colorado, when that fool Asal stopped at the farmhouse with Pollock still chasing them. But he had solved that by hiding behind the barn during the confusion, then taking the farmer's Lincoln to the nearest airport as soon as Pollock took off again in the van. Now, he was here, and he would be able to launch the SCUD himself.

Gerhardt smiled. He had made the Istad Itar ruse work for him. It was almost over, and when it was, he'd be rich. He would be the "favorite son" of Saddam Hussein, and the Iraqi madman would want him to quarterback every new and insane whim that crossed his mind.

The German carefully cut a piece of steak with his knife and fork and raised it to his mouth. He had no intention of sticking around Baghdad, however. It was retirement time. He had already found a quiet little island in the Caribbean where he could slip into a carefully created identity and spend the rest of his life sipping wine and fondling the breasts of the local native girls.

He felt the floor beneath him rock lightly. He looked at his wineglass and saw the red liquid inside threatening to tip over the side. He steadied the glass with both hands, waited for the rocking to quiet down, then looked across the table at the man seated there.

Hamid Kanafani knew about Gerhardt's part in the oil-field phase of the double strike. But neither Kanafani nor anyone else, including Saddam Hussein himself, knew that Gerhardt had made sure that Pollock found the oil-field sites. It had been necessary to hedge his bets a bit. Had he not been able to escape custody, he would have had to rely on the American's promise of freedom in return for his help in stopping the oil fires.

Gerhardt and Kanafani had barely spoken during the meal, and he decided a little conversation might be in order. "So, there are no problems?" he asked. "Everything is ready?"

Kanafani looked up. "Our timing should be perfect. The fact is, we have been far luckier than it appears *you* have been." His eyes stayed on Gerhardt's face, where the bruises Pollock had given him had turned a mixture of black, blue and yellow.

Gerhardt's hand moved to the puffiness under one eye. "We must all be ready to make sacrifices." He took another bite, washed it down with more wine, then shrugged. "It was little enough to give up for the cause." Like the knee, his face still hurt, but it too had been a small price to pay for what Saddam was paying him.

"I did not mean your face," Hamid said. "Your leg. I understand you were injured in Germany. And I noticed you still limping."

Gerhardt shrugged. "This, too, shall pass."

A man clad in a short white waiter's jacket appeared with a fresh bottle of wine, popped the cork with a silver corkscrew and left it on the table.

"What of the SCUD itself? Where do we stand?" Gerhardt asked as he poured himself another glass.

"It has been assembled. It will take only seconds to activate as soon as we are there. That is not a problem. But there are things that are. Things with *you*, old friend."

Gerhardt looked up. "Yes? Then this is the time to clear the air." He smiled as he raised his glass again. The wine was relaxing him, almost making him giddy. He would finish this glass and no more.

"There can be no doubt that there is a traitor in our midst. The counterstrikes in Oklahoma were a disaster."

"Yes," the German agreed, sobering suddenly.

Kanafani smiled wickedly. "And it could have been only *you*, Willem."

Gerhardt didn't respond.

"You were the only man in a position to inform the Americans. You led one of their agents to the sites?"

Gerhardt sensed what was coming, and it was not righteous indignation on his companion's part. He stared into the man's eyes and said, "More or less. It was necessary to divert the attention of the U.S. and enable us to accomplish our true objective."

Kanafani's smile widened. "We lost dozens of men last night. Oklahoma is littered with the bodies."

"Yes."

"I am guessing that Saddam knew nothing of your treachery."

"Of course not." Gerhardt shook his head. "He insisted that both strikes could be successful. But then Saddam is no strategist. He has proved that time and time again." He paused, frowning, then said, "But tell me, Hamid. What is it you are leading toward?"

"The fact that you purposely sabotaged the oil-field strikes without our benefactor's knowledge. And Saddam would hardly be pleased to know that." The beard shuffled into a cruel smile. "He must be kept in the dark for your safety. And he will be. For a price."

Gerhardt forced a smile. "What is that price, old friend?"

"Half of what you are getting. And do not deceive yourself. I am able to find out *exactly* what you are to be paid."

The German kept the wooden smile on his face as he nodded agreement. Lifting his steak knife and fork, he took another bite, watching Kanafani as he chewed. The man had been vital to the operation. He was the only one on board who knew the electronic sequence to activate the SCUD launcher.

Except Gerhardt himself.

Kanafani continued to leer at him across the table. "And I expect payment as soon as—" The man's words were cut off as Gerhardt suddenly shot from his chair, leaned across the table and drove the steak knife into his throat.

The terrorist's eyes opened wide in shock as blood poured from the open wound. His hands flew to the blade beneath his beard, trying to jerk it free.

Gerhardt borrowed the other man's steak knife, sat back down and finished his dinner.

Fifteen minutes later, the German had mopped up the blood and carried Kanafani to his bunk. Facing the man's severed carotid artery and pasty face toward the wall, he covered the body with a blanket.

Gerhardt tapped a button on the intercom system next to the bunk. "Mr. Kanafani has taken ill," he said into the speaker. "I will be in charge until he is feeling better. I will take over his duties with the launcher as well."

THE EXECUTIONER STARED at the video screen, watching the barns, houses, fields and trees roll by. He closes his eyes momentarily, resting them, secure in the knowledge that anything of interest he missed in the next few seconds would be picked up by the ground crew linked to the camera inside the Eagle.

The barns were what bothered him the most. Every such structure was a potential hiding place for what was officially known as a SCUD-A Battlefield Support Missile.

The warrior glanced at the fuel gauge and saw the tanks were nearing the empty mark. "Better head back, Jack," he said into the microphone in front of his face. "We're running low."

The back of Grimaldi's head nodded. The Eagle's left wing dipped as he altered course.

Bolan closed his weary eyes again as they dropped though the air toward the runways at McCord. He had spotted two flatbed trucks during the past half hour, both of them off the road and half-hidden by tall trees. The video-analysis team below had seen them too, and ground troops had been immediately dispatched to investigate.

The first truck, just inside the Pennsylvania state lane, had turned out to be a farmer helping his newlywed son and daughter-in-law move from the farm into the village of Greenscastle. The truck had suffered a flat tire , and they'd pulled off the road to fix it.

They had been predictably surprised when two teams of Delta Force commandos suddenly surrounded them at gunpoint.

The second truck had turned out to be equally innocuous. Covered by a tarp, it had been delivering coal-mining equipment to a mine site.

The wheels of the Eagle hit the runway and the plane began to slow. All of the air surveillance units had recorded similar sightings during the past several hours. Each had been checked out by the ground forces, and each had been a waste of time.

Bolan and Grimaldi waited silently as the plane re-
fueled and prepared to take off again. The warrior
took a deep breath, opened his eyes and stared at the
video screen which had gone dark. The Eagles and
Tomcats had covered the entire range within the 175-
mile launch radius three times so far. Nothing had
proved to be a viable lead, which meant the SCUD and
launcher were hidden. It wouldn't be exposed until the
last few seconds before the missile was fired, and all
the airplanes and all the high-tech equipment in the
world weren't going to find it.

The Executioner let the air out of his lungs. There
had to be a better approach to the search, some lead
to follow that would narrow the probe to manageable
proportions. And there *was* one—he could feel it in his
soul, fighting to break through his subconscious mind.

But what was it? He had seen something during the
flyovers. Or he had heard something from Asal or
Gerhardt. Or he had felt, or touched something that
was the key to this whole mission.

But what was it?

"Permission to take off," the warrior heard Grimaldi say in his ears. A moment later, they were taxi-
ing back toward the runway.

Bolan reviewed what he knew about the SCUDs
Iraq had used during the Gulf War. Soviet-made me-
dium-range missiles, crude by today's standards, limited range, remarkably poor accuracy—but deadly to
whatever they did hit. They were designed to strike at
targets such as marshaling areas, major storage dumps
and airfields behind enemy lines. They could be

launched from either permanent or mobile launching units, with land or amphibious launch capability.

As the launch information popped into the warrior's mind, the adrenaline suddenly flowed through his veins. He tapped several buttons, and the screen in front of him lighted up with a colored map of the 175-mile launch radius around Washington. His gaze fell on the blue area east of the capital city.

Amphibious launch capability. While they had planes even now flying over the Atlantic and Chesapeake and Delaware bays, the primary focus had been on land. Why? Because the missiles aimed at Israel and Saudi Arabia had been launched from land. So far as the Executioner knew, Iraq had no history of shooting SCUDs from aboard ship.

Which meant one of two things: either they weren't confident in an amphibious launching, or they just hadn't gotten around to it yet. If the latter was the case, now would be the perfect time to give it a try.

Bolan waited until the Eagle was back in the air, then spoke again into the mouth mike. "Get ready to change course, Jack."

The pilot had been with him on too many missions to be surprised. His only answer was another nod.

"Striker to McCord ground control," Bolan said into the radio. "Come in, McCord."

The same voice he'd spoken to earlier came back. "Go ahead, Striker."

"We're pulling off our sector search," the Executioner said. "Permission to change to..." He glanced down at the map, then read a set of coordinates.

The voice came back with a cocky ring in it. "Permission denied, Striker. Assignments have been made. I've been given no authorization to change—" The sentence stopped suddenly.

A few seconds later, Hal Brognola's voice replaced the air-traffic controller's. "What have you got, Striker?" the G-man asked.

"Just a hunch, Hal."

Brognola had seen the Executioner's hunches pay off too many times in the past to hesitate. "Follow it up," he barked.

A moment later, the controller's voice came back on, more meekly this time. "Permission granted, Striker. Proceed."

The Executioner tapped more buttons, and the map disappeared on the computer screen. The video camera reappeared, and he watched the buildings of Washington, D.C., fly by as Grimaldi headed east toward the Atlantic Ocean.

12

The dark green water around the shores lightened to a bright blue as Grimaldi flew the F-15 Eagle farther out over the Atlantic Ocean.

The Executioner hit the mike. "Any word yet on the Patriots?" he asked.

"Getting closer," the voice from ground control replied.

Bolan stared at the screen as the video camera recorded the rolling waves thirty thousand feet below. They neared a freighter with Norwegian markings, and he zoomed the camera slightly. There was no need for Grimaldi to drop lower. The electronic wizardry of the computer-based camera picked up everything it was capable of getting.

The warrior saw several men and a variety of crates on the deck of the Norwegian ship, but none of the wooden boxes was large enough to conceal a SCUD or launcher. He settled back as the screen turned ocean blue again.

The Eagle flew on. Bolan reached up and rubbed his bloodshot eyes with both hands. After refueling, he had directed Grimaldi northeast from Washington, over Philadelphia and Trenton, then to the very edge of the 175-mile radius near Freehold, New Jersey. They had followed the curve south over Lakewood, then Seaside Park before the ocean had appeared. Bolan had ordered Grimaldi to follow the shoreline first, guessing that whatever ship carried the SCUD might have already taken refuge in port. He had seen everything from tankers to sailboats, but nothing that caught either his eyes, nor those of the watch team on the ground below.

Upon arriving at the southern tip of the launch radius they had headed back north, concentrating the video search farther out to sea in the shipping lanes. And for the last hour and a half they had once again seen every type of seagoing vessel imaginable.

But nothing that looked as if it might bear a SCUD missile.

The screen picked up a passenger ship, and the Executioner watched the autofocus adjust itself. Along the bow, he saw a cartoon pelican emblem and the letters DFDS—a Danish cruise line. His eyes scanned the deck. Unless the components for both the SCUD and the launcher were hidden below, this wasn't the ship.

Bolan checked the longitude. The ship was on course too far south, probably to one or more of the islands in the Caribbean. And even if it changed that course immediately, it would take it too long to reach the coast area of the U.S.

The fact was, no ship this far east was going to be the one they were looking for.

"We're too far out, Jack, " Bolan said into the mike. "Let's head back in."

"You got it, Striker," Grimaldi said, and the Eagle began to bank.

Bolan tapped the buttons, calling up a map of the eastern seaboard on a screen next to the video camera's. His theory so far had been that if they hadn't already docked somewhere along the coast, the Istad Itar terrorists would stay out of American waters until the last minute, sailing shallowly into launch range, then making an about-face back into the Atlantic before the SCUD even struck. But there was a third option, too.

The warrior frowned as he studied the map. When you got right down to it, firing a SCUD wasn't much more complex than firing a bazooka, and even had a lot in common with a standard firearm. Certain basic rules of marksmanship held true, one of them being that the closer you were, the better your chances of hitting what you aimed at.

The Executioner's eyes moved back across the map to Washington. The closest accessible water that linked easily to the Atlantic was Chesapeake Bay. The closest area within the bay would be just east of Annapolis, the city the United States Naval Academy called home.

Bolan's frown deepened. The water near the academy would be well protected with naval security. But cargo ships and other seagoing traffic passed through the area daily on their way to Baltimore and other ports.

Getting that close to the target would take guts, but the terrorists had proved they were willing to take chances.

The Executioner glanced back to the screen and saw the blue waters darken to green once more as they neared the coast. What he had now was a hunch on a hunch. For all he knew, he could have been wrong with the whole sea-launch idea to begin with. The SCUD might even now be rolling out of a barn near York, Pennsylvania, or Fredericksburg, Virginia.

He pushed the negativity from his mind. The warrior had chosen his course. All he could do now was follow it.

His weary eyes returned again to the screen.

WILLEM GERHARDT MOUNTED the ladder to the deck of the freighter, passed through the superstructure and walked across the deck. The moisture in the air hadn't done his leg any good. It ached like the fires of hell as he limped painfully toward the rail.

The German grasped the rail, shifting his weight to the other leg. Slowly the burn around his knee subsided. He stared across the water as the city of Baltimore, Maryland, appeared.

A half-forgotten memory surfaced suddenly. He had been to Baltimore years earlier. It had been the year the Baltimore baseball team—what was its nickname?—had won the World Series. He and Carlos had been in the stadium early in the summer, planted a bomb near the Maryland governor's private box, then stayed to watch both the game and the explosion.

It had been the first baseball game he had ever seen. He liked the strategy involved—the secret signals the third-base coach flashed to batters and base runners, and the smooth precision involved in double plays. The signals reminded him of the strategy stages of planning a strike. The double plays were like that well-planned mission being played out successfully.

Baltimore had won that day, beating the team from New York, and executing two double plays. But his and Carlos's "double play" had been busted. An alert Baltimore policeman working game security had discovered the bomb, and an explosive squad had disarmed it.

Salt spray blew into Gerhardt's face as he watched the docks draw nearer. He shrugged at the memory. Freedom fighting, or terrorism, whatever you wanted to call it, *was* a lot like baseball. You won some, you lost some and some got rained out. The bomb meant for the governor of Maryland had been one of those that fell victim to the rain.

Gerhardt's lips widened in a smile, showing his even row of white teeth as more drizzle assaulted his face. They had been rained out that day years ago, but today he would win. And tomorrow, his career as a terrorist would be over. He would have more than enough money to be set up for life, and he would retire and disappear just as Carlos had done.

The ship pulled into port and Gerhardt turned, watching the crewmen as they began to unload several of the flatbed trucks. He had centered the entire SCUD attack around this freighter. It had been a simple matter of finding a ship that transported flatbed trucks up and down the coast to dealers, modifying another flatbed to fit the launcher, then getting several of his men infiltrated into the crew. They had hijacked the *Ginger Juliette* once it was at sea, and killed the rest of the crew. Istad Itar's own ship had drawn alongside two nights earlier and loaded the SCUD on board, then disappeared back into the Atlantic.

The German's gaze fell on the bright blue Chevrolet flatbed in the center of the deck. Beneath the tarp, the launcher waited. They would be less than forty miles from Washington when they passed Annapolis, and while they were unlikely to actually hit the White House or other government buildings, the close range would virtually assure that the missile struck somewhere in Washington proper—the very heart of the United States.

Even if they missed the whole D.C. area, the chemical warhead would spread its death up and down the coast, and perhaps for several miles farther inland. Many people would die. Even more important, their deaths would mean a great psychological victory over the Americans.

But most important of all was the victory it represented for Willem Gerhardt.

Gerhardt watched as the crew drove the last few trucks down the ramp onto the docks. He glanced at his wrist. They would leave port again in two hours, just as soon as the paperwork was complete. The mission's success had come from the ship's appearance of legitimacy, and this was no time to change a shipping schedule that might leave loose ends that could prevent the ship from reaching the launch point. Of course the launcher was primed and ready, and if need be, he could shoot the SCUD from its current position. But he would prefer a better chance at the White

House. While the chemical warhead would be just as deadly from here, the psychological ramifications would be far more reaching if they struck the American capital.

The German turned back to the rail, looking up over the dock toward the Baltimore skyline. What a shame it was. It was summer. Baseball season. The Orioles might well be at home, playing the Yankees again.

And there would be no time to catch the game.

VIDEO SHOTS of the Cape Charles area flashed across the screen as Grimaldi steered the Eagle toward the entrance to Chesapeake Bay.

Bolan had been without sleep for two nights now, and his eyes burned as he watched the images pass by. The Eagle dipped slightly, and the Chesapeake Bay Bridge-Tunnel appeared. A moment later, the Executioner was watching large ships and smaller craft as they came and went on the intercoastal waterway.

Speaking into the face mike again, he said, "Slow her down, Jack. Let's get as good a look as we can."

The roar of the engines lowered as Grimaldi cut speed.

Radio traffic came over the headset as Bolan continued to study the screen. A moment later, he heard a familiar voice.

"McCord ground control to Striker. Come in, Striker."

"I'm listening, Hal."

"Where are you, big guy?"

"We're just entering the mouth of the bay," the Executioner replied. "Nothing to report yet. I'll make contact just as soon as I see anything."

"No, Striker," Brognola said. "I've got something for *you.* You might want to hustle Jack on north. One of the Navy planes just zeroed in on a freighter nearing Baltimore. Said it looked like they were transporting a load of trucks. Flatbed trucks. Remember the mobile launchers Saddam used in the Gulf?"

Bolan paused. He had set Grimaldi off on a systematic course to cover the entire bay area, with heavy emphasis on the waterway near Annapolis. But if somebody else had seen something, there was no sense wasting time. "What did the ground crew think?" he asked Brognola.

"They've run the tape back three times. The trucks have tarps over them. That's not unusual—helps keep the sea salt off the paint jobs during transport."

"If they're covered how do you know they're flatbeds?" Bolan asked.

"That's where it gets interesting," Brognola stated. "One of the tarps blew off as the Tomcat got close. The crew seemed a little too anxious to hurry it back on to just save a paint job."

Bolan keyed the mike again. "Do you have another plane that can fly this end of the bay?" he asked.

"That's affirmative. There's one down refueling at Langley right now. I'll have them change his course as soon as he's in the air."

"Roger, Hal."

The Executioner waited a second, then said, "You hear the man, Jack?"

"Affirmative, Striker."

"Then what are we waiting for?"

Grimaldi's answer was to gun the Eagle back to top speed.

A few minutes later, the engines slowed again. Bolan watched the tiny cities of Severna Park and Glen Burnie pass on the shore. The Eagle passed slowly over several small boats, then a large freighter appeared on the screen, slowly making its way toward Baltimore.

"You read me, Striker?" Brognola said in the Executioner's ear.

"I've got you, Hal. That it on the monitor?"

"That's it."

Bolan studied the ship as they flew over. Objects "truck size and shape" were indeed parked bumper to bumper along the deck. And if the Tomcat "alligator" and ground crew had seen a flatbed truck earlier, then flatbed trucks were what those objects had to be.

But so what? That didn't mean a SCUD launcher was hidden in their midst.

The Eagle passed over the ship. "Hit a one-eighty, Jack," Bolan said. "I want another look."

Then to Brognola, "Anybody checked out the ship yet, Hal? Registration? All that?"

"Just got it back," the big Fed replied. Bolan heard the rustle of paper being torn from a printer, then, "The *Ginger Juliette* made a scheduled port call late last night in Norfolk. Unloaded eleven vehicles." Brognola blew air between his lips in disgust. "Maybe it *is* legitimate. Maybe we're down to the point of grasping at straws."

The Eagle slowed as it flew back over the ship. Bolan's bloodshot eyes studied the monitor. On the screen, he could even see tiny figures walking on deck. The ship's crew. Too far away to make out their faces, but he could still recognize movement.

The Executioner was about to speak into the mike again when a new form exited the superstructure at the center of the ship. He watched it walk across the deck, his stomach muscles tightening with every step the figure took. Except for one small irregularity, it looked no different on the screen than the other figures moving about the deck.

But that small deviation happened to be a pronounced limp.

The plane passed over the ship again. "One more time, Jack," the Executioner said. "Turn her around."

Grimaldi didn't hesitate in carrying out the order. The ace pilot had been a good soldier far too long for that. But the Stony Man pilot had never been anyone's "yes man," either, and had never hesitated to voice an opinion when he didn't agree with a tactic.

"We're heading back, Striker," he said, "but I got to tell you. I'm pretty damn familiar with video air surveillance. We're not going to see anything we haven't seen already."

"I couldn't agree with you more," Bolan said as they neared the port of Baltimore.

"Then why do you want me to—" Grimaldi broke off the thought when the canopy behind him flew open and the ejection seat sent Bolan flying up into the sky behind the Eagle.

The warrior pulled the chute as the Eagle flew on, letting it flower out over his head and halt his fall. He looked down to see the harbor area. The *Ginger Juliette* had docked next to one of the loading terminals.

The Executioner let the sea wind blow him inland as he descended. Somehow, he had to find a way to slip onto the ship. That would involve keeping a low profile, and dropping out of the sky onto the deck was hardly what he had in mind.

A half mile from the water, he looked down to see what appeared to be a residential area. He'd be noticed there as well, but he could lose any curious pursuers on his way back to the harbor.

The Executioner watched the tiny specks on the ground grow larger as he descended—and they watched him. By the time he reached the top of the tall tenement houses along the crowded Baltimore street, a crowd of at least thirty people had bunched together to look up and point at the sky.

Bolan came down in the middle of a street amid the cheers of a crowd who obviously thought it was some sort of promotional gimmick. A half-dozen children surrounded the Executioner as he hauled in his chute.

"That was great, mister!" shouted one little boy.

"Do it again! Do it again!" screamed another.

A little girl demanded his autograph.

Bolan shrugged out of the harness and dropped the chute to the concrete as car tires suddenly squealed to a halt behind him. The crowd in front of him quieted, their faces showing instant fear.

The Executioner turned to see a silver Mercedes two feet away. The doors opened and four men in the colors of some local gang stepped out.

The driver, wearing a yellow bandana over his head and sporting a mangy goatee, stepped up to Bolan and studied him head to foot. "Fly-boy, you jump out of the sky into *my* hood, you better have a damn good reason."

"I do," Bolan said. "I'm trying to save your life." He drew the Desert Eagle, rapped it across the gang leader's temple, then turned it on the other three punks as the man slithered to the ground. "Get down next to your buddy," he ordered.

Smiles replaced the frightened looks on the faces of the crowd. People began to clap again as the three gang members hit the concrete.

Bolan found the keys still in the Mercedes' ignition and jumped behind the wheel. The smell of burned rubber filled the air as he spun away from the crowd and down the street toward the harbor.

Three minutes later, the scent of salt sea filled the Executioner's nostrils. He saw the customhouse, then a passenger terminal. Crossing a quayside railway, he pulled into the parking lot of a four-story office building and got out.

The *Ginger Juliette* had docked at the loading terminal two hundred feet away.

On the deck of the ship, their hands gripping the rail and watching the dock, Bolan saw at least twenty hard-looking seamen. All wore either light jackets or baggy shirts—the type of dress men wear to hide guns in warm weather.

Near the center of the row of armed terrorists, staring off over the city of Baltimore, his face immersed in thought, was Willem Gerhardt.

The Executioner moved quickly behind a stack of containers waiting to be loaded onto another ship. He watched the first of several flatbed trucks, driven by a dark-skinned man, roll down onto the quay ramp before moving on across the terminal toward a small loading office next to a transit shed.

Bolan kept low behind the containers, making his way toward the office. Sprinting the last few yards to the door, he kept his eyes on Gerhardt.

The German was caught up in some thought as he stared out over the city. He paid no attention as the Executioner entered the office.

The secretary's desk in the one-room building stood empty. But a tall slender man with long hair sat behind a desk against the wall, holding a magazine with a nude woman on the cover. He wore olive green work pants and a matching shirt that announced to the world his name was "Mitch." He glanced up as Bolan entered the building.

The Executioner looked him up and down, much like the gangster had done Bolan a few moments earlier. The shirt and pants would be tight, but they would have to do.

The warrior walked to the desk, drew the Desert Eagle and shoved it under the man's nose. "Take off your clothes," he ordered.

Complete and absolute fear consumed Mitch's face. The magazine fell from his hands onto the desk.

Bolan suppressed a chuckle and shook his head. "Don't worry," he said, nodding to the magazine. "I like girls as much as the next guy. Just give me your clothes and I'll get out of your way."

The man's face told Bolan he still wasn't convinced as he began to unbutton his shirt.

The Executioner waited. His plan was to hurry into the olive drab dockworker's uniform, grab the nearest clipboard and make his way onto the *Ginger Juliette* with a story about paperwork problems.

That plan changed as the door to the building suddenly opened.

The warrior turned to see the man who had driven the flatbed truck off the ship standing openmouthed in surprise.

"There's been a change of plan," Bolan interrupted, motioning him toward the wall with the big .44. He hurried over to the man, shook him down and came up with a compact Smith & Wesson 9 mm automatic.

Bolan ordered the Istad Itar terrorist facedown on the floor as Mitch finished undressing. A moment later, the warrior was squeezing into the tight uniform. "Stay where you are for the next five minutes," he told Mitch, who now stood sheepishly in his underwear. "Call the cops if you want. But don't go outside unless you want to take the chance of catching a bullet."

The gulp that went down the thin man's long throat looked like a python swallowing a elephant.

Bolan turned to the terrorist on the floor. "Get up," he demanded. When the man was on his feet, he said, "Who's in charge of the launch?"

The hardman shook his head. "I know nothing of—"

The Executioner knew he had no time to waste. He placed the muzzle of the Desert Eagle against the terrorist's temple and cocked the hammer.

"Everybody deserves a second chance," Bolan said. "Same question. Try again. Screw up, and you'll have a bullet in your brain."

"Captain Kanafani was in charge. But he is sick. Gerhardt is to launch the missile."

"What in the hell is—" Mitch said behind the Executioner. A quick glare from the warrior stopped him in midsentence.

Bolan hauled the terrorist back to his feet. "Keep your hands at your side and act natural," he said. "We're going on board the ship, and you're going to take me to Gerhardt. You got it?"

The man nodded. The Executioner shoved the Desert Eagle into the back of his pants, then pushed the terrorist toward the door. They crossed the terminal, and a moment later started up the ramp to the *Ginger Juliette*.

The Executioner's eyes scanned the deck. Gerhardt had moved farther along the rail toward the bow. Still staring out over the city of Baltimore, he stood less than a hundred feet from the only tarp-covered truck still on the ship.

The SCUD missile and mobile launcher.

Bolan pushed the man in front of him up the ramp. They were three feet from the ship when the German turned and looked along the rail.

Gerhardt leaned forward, squinting into the night. Then the squint vanished as he recognized the man in the tight olive green work clothes. He turned on his heel and started toward the tarp-covered SCUD launcher.

The Executioner shoved the man in front of him onto the deck, where he sprawled full length. Drawing the Desert Eagle from behind his back, Bolan brought it up and dropped the sights on Gerhardt's back.

As his finger moved back on the trigger, a man wearing bell-bottom sailor's jeans drew a small submachine pistol from under his blue chambray shirt and stepped away from the rail—directly into the Executioner's line of fire.

Bolan followed through on the trigger, letting the big .44 Magnum round rip through the blue shirt and drive the man to the deck. His hand followed the mighty recoil upward, his finger preparing to squeeze the trigger again as soon as Gerhardt returned to his sights. But by the time the gun fell back in line, the rest of the men had moved away from the rail and produced weapons of their own.

The warrior hit the deck, diving to his belly under a barrage of fire that sailed along the rail. He felt the tight shirt rip across the shoulders as he rolled over, fired and dropped the nearest man, then rolled again as a new assault of bullets drilled into the deck where he'd lain.

Coming to a halt on his belly again, Bolan squeezed the trigger, dropping a man wearing corduroy jeans and a windbreaker. The .44 threw the terrorist back into a comrade behind him, who sported a Greek fisherman's cap and held a nickel-plated revolver in both hands. The Greek's finger tightened involuntarily on the trigger, and the terrorist in the windbreaker took a .357 slug in the back, as well.

Bolan let him fall out of the way, then double-tapped two rounds into the chest of the Greek fisherman. The Executioner rolled across the deck, slamming up against the superstructure, then swung the Desert Eagle into target acquisition and tapped a round into an Istad Itar gunner who had produced a MAC-10.

The Magnum hollowpoint drove the man back two steps. His hands flew over his head, and a full-auto burst of 9 mm rounds shot harmlessly toward the heavens. The man fell forward onto his face and the subgun skidded across the deck.

The terrorist Bolan had escorted from the dock office suddenly dived forward, grasping for the subgun. The Executioner fired a .44 bullet into his nape.

Three more shots took out three more gunners. Bolan dropped the magazine from the Desert Eagle and shoved a fresh load into the grips.

The "blockade" between Gerhardt and the Executioner parted momentarily. Bolan swung the big .44 toward the German, who still limped toward the SCUD launcher at the other end of the ship. He squeezed the trigger and saw the terrorist go down.

But more than a dozen men remained and stood firing their weapons. The Executioner dived behind a lifeboat as full-auto fire followed him across the deck. He leaned back against the cool metal of the tiny craft as bullets tore blindly through the hull.

The warrior caught his breath, then drew the Beretta with his left hand. Flipping the selector to 3-round-burst mode, he leaped back around the barrier, firing with both hands.

The big Desert Eagle hammered two rounds of semijacketed hollowpoints into the belly and chest of a man wearing a green sweatshirt. The Beretta burped a trio of smaller 9 mm slugs that tore off the face of a gunman toting a Browning Hi-Power.

The Executioner swung the massive .44 Magnum to the left, letting its business end fall in line with a long-haired terrorist in sunglasses. The Desert Eagle boomed, and another round split the spectacles in half at the nose before drilling into the gunman's brain. The sawed-off double-barreled shotgun in his lifeless hands clattered to the deck.

At the same time, Bolan's left hand wasted no time. Another 3-round burst from the Beretta caved in the breastbone of an Istad Itar terrorist wearing a jean jacket. The warrior squeezed the trigger again, took out a hardman with a matched set of gold earrings.

Only three terrorists stood on the deck. One aimed a Para-Ordnance high-capacity P-14 his way, spraying a burst and praying that one of his wild .45s might hit. The second was trying to clear the stovepipe jam from his Walther P-88.

The third man faced away from the Executioner, limping painfully toward the SCUD launcher farther down the deck. Both of his hands were pressed against a bullet hole in his side as he staggered toward the tarp.

Bolan stood, took careful aim with the Desert Eagle and dropped a .44 Magnum between the eyes of the man with the Para-Ordnance. He flipped the Beretta back to semiauto and brought it up in line with the man trying to clear the stovepipe. A lone 9 mm round entered the hardman's cranium just below his left eye.

The Executioner walked forward as the last two Istad Itar gunmen fell to his fire. His footsteps clicked hollowly over the deck as he stepped over the bodies and made his way down the rail.

The German had reached the SCUD launcher and pulled off the tarp when Bolan stopped ten feet behind him. The warrior saw the missile, loaded and ready to be raised and launched.

Gerhardt turned around, his face displaying the same cocky smile Bolan had first seen when they'd met in Okarchie, Oklahoma. The terrorist's breath came in wheezes as blood poured from the open wound in his side. "Three more seconds." He coughed, and blood spurted from his lips as he spoke. "Three more seconds...and I would have had the missile in the air."

"I doubt it."

The German forced the smile to grow wider. "Shall we see?"

Bolan nodded. "Go ahead."

Gerhardt turned back toward the SCUD, then whirled, a .45 clutched in one hand.

"One, two, three," the Executioner said, and split the man's spine with a .44 Magnum hollowpoint. He walked forward as the terrorist fell to his back on the deck.

Gerhardt stared up at him, the cocky smile finally gone as he struggled for his last breaths. "You counted...too fast..." he grunted, then died.

The Executioner stepped over the dead crewmen of the *Ginger Juliette* and entered the superstructure of the ghost ship. He climbed the ladder to the radio-room, sat down in the chair and picked up the sea phone. A moment later, he had Hal Brognola on the line in Washington.

"Hang tight, big guy" were Brognola's first words. "The Patriots are up and ready."

**Blazing a perilous trail through the
heart of darkness**

JAMES AXLER
DEATH LANDS®

Road Wars

A cryptic message sends Ryan Cawdor and the Armorer on an
odyssey to the Pacific Northwest, away from their band of warrior
survivalists. As the endless miles come between them, the odds for
survival are not in their favor.

In the Deathlands, fate and chance are clashing with
frightening force.

Take
4 explosive books
plus a
mystery bonus
FREE

Mail to: Gold Eagle Reader Service
3010 Walden Ave.
P.O. Box 1394
Buffalo, NY 14240-1394

YEAH! Rush me 4 FREE Gold Eagle novels and my FREE mystery gift.
Then send me 4 brand-new novels every other month as they come off
the presses. Bill me at the low price of just $14.80* for each shipment—
a saving of 12% off the cover prices for all four books! There is NO extra
charge for postage and handling! There is no minimum number of books I
must buy. I can always cancel at any time simply by returning a shipment
at your cost or by returning any shipping statement marked "cancel." Even
if I never buy another book from Gold Eagle, the 4 free books and surprise
gift are mine to keep forever.

164 BPM ANQY

Name _____ (PLEASE PRINT) _____

Address _____ Apt. No. _____

City _____ State _____ Zip _____

Signature (if under 18, parent or guardian must sign)

* Terms and prices subject to change without notice. Sales tax applicable in
  NY. This offer is limited to one order per household and not valid to
  present subscribers. Offer not available in Canada.

AC-94

**Don't miss out on the action in these titles featuring
THE EXECUTIONER®, ABLE TEAM® and PHOENIX FORCE®!**

SuperBolan

#61434 TAKEDOWN $4.99 ☐
War has come back to the Old World, carried out by a former Romanian
Securitate Chief and his army of professional killers.

#61435 DEATH'S HEAD $4.99 ☐
While in Berlin on a Mafia search-and-destroy, Bolan uncovers a covert
cadre of Soviets working with German neo-Nazis and other right-wing nation-
alists.

Stony Man™

#61892 STONY MAN VIII $4.99 ☐
A power-hungry industrialist fuels anarchy in South America.

#61893 STONY MAN #9 STRIKEPOINT $4.99 ☐
Free-lance talent from the crumbling Russian empire fuels Iraq's nuclear
power.

#61894 STONY MAN #10 SECRET ARSENAL $4.99 ☐
A biochemical weapons conspiracy puts America in the hot seat.

(limited quantities available on certain titles)

TOTAL AMOUNT	$
POSTAGE & HANDLING	$
($1.00 for one book, 50¢ for each additional)	
APPLICABLE TAXES*	$ _____
TOTAL PAYABLE	$ _____

(check or money order—please do not send cash)

To order, complete this form and send it, along with a check or money order for
the total above, payable to Gold Eagle Books, to: **In the U.S.:** 3010 Walden Avenue,
P.O. Box 9077, Buffalo, NY 14269-9077; **In Canada:** P.O. Box 636, Fort Erie, Ontario,
L2A 5X3.

Name: _____

Address: _____ City: _____

State/Prov.: _____ Zip/Postal Code: _____

*New York residents remit applicable sales taxes.
Canadian residents remit applicable GST and provincial taxes.

GEBACK7A

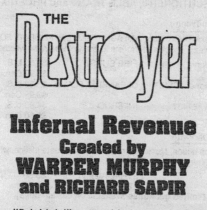

**Don't miss out on the action in these titles featuring
THE EXECUTIONER®, ABLE TEAM® and PHOENIX FORCE®!**

The Terror Trilogy

Features Mack Bolan, along with ABLE TEAM and PHOENIX FORCE, as they
battle neo-Nazis and Arab terrorists to prevent war in the Middle East.

The Executioner #61186	FIRE BURST	$3.50 U.S.	☐
		$3.99 Can.	☐
The Executioner #61187	CLEANSING FLAME	$3.50 U.S.	☐
		$3.99 Can.	☐
SuperBolan #61437	INFERNO	$4.99 U.S.	☐
		$5.50 Can.	☐

The Executioner®

With nonstop action, Mack Bolan represents ultimate justice, within or
beyond the law.

#61182	LETHAL AGENT	$3.50	☐
#61183	CLEAN SWEEP	$3.50	☐

(limited quantities available on certain titles)

TOTAL AMOUNT	$
POSTAGE & HANDLING	$
($1.00 for one book, 50¢ for each additional)	
APPLICABLE TAXES*	$ _____
TOTAL PAYABLE	$ _____

(check or money order—please do not send cash)

To order, complete this form and send it, along with a check or money order for
the total above, payable to Gold Eagle Books, to: **In the U.S.:** 3010 Walden Avenue,
P.O. Box 9077, Buffalo, NY 14269-9077; **In Canada:** P.O. Box 636, Fort Erie, Ontario,
L2A 5X3.

Name: _____

Address: _____ City: _____

State/Prov.: _____ Zip/Postal Code: _____

*New York residents remit applicable sales taxes.
Canadian residents remit applicable GST and provincial taxes.

GEBACK7